"Rouff has a chance to be to Vegas what Carl Hiaasen is to Florida."

—Tod Goldberg, author of *Gangsterland*

"The story of young love, a cross-country road trip, a haunted house, and a war with a corrupt casino owner—all captured with the depth and detail only a genuine Las Vegas insider can deliver."

—Megan Edwards, author of *Getting off on Frank Sinatra*

"Anna Christiansen takes on City Hall in this gripping Sin City story. Her mission in *The House Always Wins* is a classic tale that's equally suspenseful, well-written, and memorable. Author Brian Rouff keeps the pages turning as he pulls out all the stops in his latest Las Vegas novel."

—Cathy Scott, author of *The Killing of Tupac Shakur* and *Murder of a Mafia Daughter*

"Brian Rouff has done it. Again. His ability to weave in humor, mystery, and drama with iconic Las Vegas history makes readers feel like they've been given a winning poker hand. *The House Always Wins* had me giggling and smiling and turning the pages as fast as I could."

—Jami Carpenter, Executive Producer and host of Vegas PBS' "Book Club."

"Rouff takes fact, mixes it with a bit of fiction, and stirs it into a wonderful cocktail. It's a terrific ride through Vegas old and new."

—Paul Atreides, author of the "World of Deadheads" novels

"Brian Rouff's ability to get inside his characters while examining universal truths is outstanding. *The House Always Wins* is funny, poignant, and builds a bridge between the yesterdays, todays, and tomorrows that make up our lives.

—Bob Burris, writer/producer "1000 to 1."

~O~

"A page-turner with a humorous twist you won't want to put down."

—Morgan St. James, author of *A Corpse in the Soup*

~O~

"Las Vegas is a city of ghosts. Some apparitions haunt its mobbed-up past. Others seem to walk among us. Author Brian Rouff understands Las Vegas and its ghosts better than most, and it shows in his latest novel. *The House Always Wins* is entertaining and intriguing and will make a great addition to your Las Vegas bookshelf."

—John L. Smith, author of *Of Rats and Men* and *Even a Street Dog*

~O~

"A love story. Vegas. A house with deadly secrets. Brian Rouff does it again with *The House Always Wins*."

—Gretchen Archer, author of the *Davis Way Crime Caper Series*

~O~

"Once again, Brian Rouff has created a masterful cast of diverse characters. Readers will enjoy the wit, style, imagination, and intrigue in this unusual and compelling novel set in Las Vegas."

—Stephen Murray, author of *Murder Aboard the Queen Elizabeth II*

THE HOUSE ALWAYS WINS

❧ Also by Brian Rouff ❧

Dice Angel
Money Shot
Restless City

THE HOUSE ALWAYS WINS

BRIAN ROUFF

HUNTINGTON PRESS
LAS VEGAS, NEVADA

The House Always Wins

Published by
Huntington Press
3665 Procyon Street
Las Vegas, NV 89103
Phone (702) 252-0655
e-mail: books@huntingtonpress.com

ISBN: 978-1-944877-06-4
$16.95US

Production & Design: Laurie Cabot

Cover Design: Laurie Cabot, Tanya Maynard, Maile Austraw

Cover Photos: Charleville Castle staircase: Christina Welbourne; ©123rf.com: Cigar in ashtray, joebelanger; Fedora, stokkete; Smoke, Warongdech Thaiwatcharamas; Man on stairs, Ysbrand Cosijn

❧ DEDICATION ❧

To my father, for all the stories.
And to the grandkids, who finally
get a chance to hear them.

ACKNOWLEDGEMENTS

Other than filmmaking, I can't think of a more collaborative medium than creating a book. A couple dozen people or more contributed greatly to this project.

To my first readers: Gretchen Archer, Bob Burris, Cynthia Carbajal, Megan Edwards, Nikki Igbo, Steve Lake, Rebecca Ioane, Stephen Murray, and Steve Zieman. I can always count on you for insight, inspiration, and tough love. I'll be happy to return the favor any time.

To Megan Neri, Melissa Biernacinski, Tiffannie Bond, Meagan McCall and the rest of the Millennials and Gen Xers at Imagine Communications who patiently answered endless versions of my question, "Do young people say (or do or know) this?"

To Deke Castleman, simply the best editor in the business. You make everything better.

To Laurie Cabot for the ghostly cover design and everything between the covers.

To Maile Austraw for the fine-artist's assist on the cover.

To Bob Burris and Bill Klein for the song lyrics. I could never write a song if my life depended on it.

To Geoff Schumacher and the Las Vegas Mob Museum, where I spent lots of quality research time.

To my sister, Trudy Altman, still my biggest fan.

To my daughters, Emmy and Amanda, who inadvertently helped make Anna a living, breathing, human being.

And, as always, to Tammy.

PROLOGUE

Dear Auntie:

I don't even know how to begin to apologize for not writing or calling or even posting on your Facebook account these last difficult months. I'm afraid I hurt your feelings and I hope you know I never intended to.

I have no excuse except to say I didn't want to worry you. And truth be known, I was scared you'd tell my parents, not that you'd be betraying my trust, but because you'd genuinely think it was the right thing to do. And the longer I waited, the harder it got. And then I had to wait till the whole fiasco was over, so I'd know how it all ended.

Finally, here we are and I need to explain everything. But it's such a lengthy and convoluted story, with bad guys and friendly ghosts and mayhem and murder, that I knew I had to start at the beginning and tell the whole tale exactly as it happened while it was still fresh in my mind. Little did I know it would turn into a full-blown memoir. Maybe I should have; after all, writing is what I do best.

I won't blame you if you don't read this. But I so hope you will. I know I don't have the right to ask your forgiveness. But at the very least, I need your understanding.

Thank you from the bottom of my heart. I love you more.

Your Unworthy Niece,
Anna

PART ONE

May

CHAPTER 1

On Sunday night, I woke up once an hour to look at the clock. Funny how your brain won't let you get a good night's sleep when you have a big day in store. Of course, I finally fell into a deep slumber about 30 minutes before the alarm's piercing bleet-bleet-bleet managed to work its way into my dream, materializing as the backup signal of a giant dump truck getting ready to flatten my car. I don't even want to get into *that* symbolism.

After slamming the snooze button with enough force to make me wonder if it would ever function again, I stumbled out of bed and somehow made my way to the bathroom, where the harsh fluorescent lighting accentuated every flaw and imperfection, past, present and future. Red, puffy, too-far-apart eyes? Check. Pillow marks criss-crossing my right cheek? Check. Tiny scar on my chin from a childhood jumping-on-the-couch accident? Double check. Friends and family tell me I'm a fine-looking young woman (that's how they say it), but they don't count. I'd trade a hundred of those well-meaning comments for one "hot."

Maybe in my next lifetime, I'll bargain away 20 IQ points for an extra cup size.

A steaming shower, a few drops of Visine, and some hastily applied makeup helped a little, as did the large coffee and Kind Bar I grabbed at the Stop 'n' Go. On the five-minute drive to work, I practiced my speech for the hundredth time.

"Mr. Knudsen, I've been with the paper almost two years now ..."

The first of my second thoughts. He knew how long I'd worked for the *Scandia Gazette.* Or did he? Couldn't hurt to remind him. The opening stayed. But what was the proper grammar? "Almost" or "nearly?" I'd check my AP *Stylebook* when I got there.

"I'm a good reporter. You said so yourself at my review." A review that lasted all of five minutes and resulted in a $25-a-month raise, which enabled me to add the Kind Bar to my morning routine on Mondays, Wednesdays, and Fridays.

In my mind's eye, I could see Mr. Knudsen glance at his watch impatiently.

Okay, time to speed things along. "Please don't make me cover another butter-sculpting contest or town-hall meeting."

Ick. That sounded needy. Mr. Knudsen didn't respond well to needy.

"Isn't it time you put me on a real story?"

Dummy, don't make it a question. Too easy to say "no."

How about this? "I deserve to work on a real story."

On cue, a scene from my father's favorite movie

flashed into view. Clint Eastwood telling the bad guy, "Deserve's got nothin' to do with it." Right before shooting him square between the eyes.

Now what? I thought of something yesterday. Why didn't I jot it down? Maybe I wasn't such a good reporter after all.

These unproductive thoughts swirled around my head like angry hornets as the car pulled into the parking lot. My car did that a lot—operate on automatic pilot. Darn it, I wasn't ready.

"Hey, Anna," Barbara, our receptionist, said cheerily as I walked through the front door. "Mr. Knudsen's ready for you."

No time to settle in, check the *Stylebook*, or even refill my coffee. I swallowed hard, not an easy thing to do when your mouth is dry as a sand dune. "Thanks," squeaked out a thin voice that sounded nothing like me.

Before I could announce my presence, Mr. Knudsen motioned me in without looking up from his paper. He maintained an open-door policy at all times, although most people never took advantage of it, because that meant having to actually talk to him. He was a gruff old guy with a shock of white hair that was always the same length. How he pulled that off I'll never know. The office, piled high with old newspapers and older bread crumbs, smelled like dust and cigarettes, a holdover from the days when you could smoke indoors. I sat in the one metal chair fronting an ancient desk and smoothed my skirt, trying to look professional. When he spoke, I could hardly hear the words, because of the pulse thrumming in my ears. Whatever I'd practiced went out the window in that instant.

"How old are you these days?" he asked, peering at me from under his glasses.

The question caught me off guard and I had to think for a moment. "Twenty-four. Almost twenty-five. A quarter of a century." It sounded old to me, because it was the oldest I'd ever been.

He tore his gaze away from the printout, moved his glasses to the top of his head, and fixed me with an appraising stare. "When you get to be my age, you'll start subtracting years instead of adding them."

I smiled weakly, not knowing what to say.

Clearing his throat, he continued, "So Jeremy's out sick, some kind of stomach bug, and Carol had to go to Lansing on a family emergency. Not life or death, I'm told, but we're shorthanded nonetheless. I know you're tired of all this county-fair and obituary crap and I've got nobody to cover tonight's concert at the Royal. A band called the Dickweeds. Supposedly making a name for themselves out west, though with a name like that, I wonder how. Ever hear of 'em?"

My heart gave a little flutter. They were on my Spotify rotation, a retro alt country blues band with a small horn section. "Yes, sir."

"In my day, all the groups had normal names. Grateful Dead, Pink Floyd, Lynyrd Skynyrd. Anyway, I need a review, plus a profile of the lead singer. Twelve-hundred words give or take, on my desk Wednesday morning. I'll run it front page of the Living section, above the fold. The ad department wants younger demos? I'll give 'em younger demos. Interested?"

By way of response, I jumped up, leaned across the desk, and kissed Mr. Knudsen on the cheek. He didn't look shocked exactly, but close for a man with only two expressions—gruff and gruffer.

"Can't you read the sign?" he asked, regaining his composure and pointing to a yellowing hand-lettered poster on the wall. "Do Not Touch the Editor."

"Yes, sir. Sorry, sir." My face felt like a furnace. I backed out of the room and right into a filing cabinet. It made a loud thump. "Thank you for the opportunity, sir."

"Don't let me down," he said.

A small voice told me I already had.

CHAPTER 2

Scandia, Michigan, is a city of 12,000 or so residents situated halfway between Charlevoix and Traverse City on the shores of Lake Michigan in the northern part of the state. We're not Yoopers, as residents of the Upper Peninsula (U.P., get it?) are often called, but we share a similar dialect and sensibility. Visitors sometimes make fun of our town, because they think we're named after an amusement park, but the name was ours first.

I'd lived here my whole life, which was why I didn't pay much attention to my surroundings as I traveled between points A and B. (In a town this size, that was about all the points we had.) This proved especially true that night as I steered my Ford Focus, which I bought with my own money (mostly), toward the Royal Theater on Main Street and my first plum reporting assignment.

I squeezed into a really tight spot that might or might not have been a parking space just around the block from the theater and headed toward the Royal, camera bag slung low over my shoulder (I was doing double-duty as the photographer). The

Royal, a historic white-brick three-story structure patterned after a Renaissance Danish castle, replete with domes and turrets and a little Dutch-style windmill in front that looked completely out of place, was built in 1927 when Scandia's fishing industry was booming. It survived the Depression, made a comeback after the war, enjoyed its heyday in the '50s and '60s, and closed for repairs in 1974. It didn't reopen until three years ago, when a smattering of federal stimulus money trickled our way and put our dormant construction industry back to work, at least temporarily.

Since then, the Royal had been home to performers as diverse as Garrison Keillor, the Fab Faux, the Missoula Children's Theater, local old-time favorite Mitch Ryder, the Fly-Fishing Film Tour, and a host of political types running for office. And of course, tonight's headliners, the Dickweeds. Scandia didn't normally attract up-and-coming bands like this and I was determined to find out why they chose to grace our stage at all.

Assuming I could get in. To my dismay, the line stretched all the way to the end of the block. Mr. Knudsen said my ticket would be waiting at Will Call, but the Royal didn't have a separate Will Call window, so I had to wait with the rest of the patrons. I looked around for a familiar face, but didn't see one, an oddity in a town our size. What I did notice was I seemed to be the oldest person present. Apparently, I was pushing the upper limit of the Dickweed demographic.

After a half-hour, I finally found myself at the

box-office window, where a moon-faced girl with a bored expression took way too long inspecting my ID before saying, "You're not on the list."

I felt my chest tighten. "Th-th-that's impossible," I said. "Please check again. It's important."

She gave the paper a quick once-over. "Sorry, no Anna Christiansen. Next!"

The kid behind me began to nudge me out of the way.

"Wait! I'll pay. How much?"

"Twenty-two fifty. Cash or debit?"

Hands shaking, I fumbled through my purse, extracting a ten, a five, three ones, and some assorted change that just didn't add up. And my debit card was nowhere in sight.

"Next!" the girl said again. I wanted to reach through the window and punch her in her chipmunk cheeks.

"Come on, lady, move it," said the kid behind me, who was now slouching next to me. I wanted to hit him, too.

"Okay, okay, do you have SRO tickets?" Desperate now, picturing my whole journalistic career going down in flames.

"SRO?"

"Standing room only." I crossed my fingers and prayed.

"Well, we do, way in the back of the balcony. But you won't be able to see anything."

"I don't care. How much?"

"Twelve fifty."

I pushed the change her way. A nickel fell on the sidewalk and the kid stooped to pick it up and hand it to me. Maybe I wouldn't smack him after all.

The girl continued, "But you have to sign this waiver. No refunds under any circumstances."

She thrust the form in my direction and I dashed off a hasty scrawl that looked an awful lot like "Screw You."

Clutching my ticket like a precious stone, I entered the ornate lobby and headed toward the stairway leading to the balcony. Already, I could hear the sounds of the opening number, a mid-tempo blues rocker I recognized, "I'm Sick of Me." I knew just how they felt.

CHAPTER 3

The view from SRO was worse than advertised. I'm barely five-four and not only is the entire world taller than I am, they were all standing in front of me, blocking my line of sight. Elbowing my way through the throng was out of the question; I simply didn't have enough elbows. But if I bobbed and weaved just so, I could sort of make out some of the band members between the forest of bodies, looking all shadowy and mysterious. The lanky lead-guitar player, I knew, could only be front-man and lead-singer Rob Lazarus. The rest of the band could have been extras from central casting for all I could tell.

I fished out my reporter's spiral notebook and jotted down two words for future reference: "This blows." At least the sound system worked flawlessly. I could distinguish every note and nuance, definitely helpful for knitting my review into the feature story. These guys were accomplished musicians, better live than on their recordings, with a loose precision that came, no doubt, from thousands of practice hours and hundreds of gigs in venues that made the Royal look like the Hollywood Bowl. After their set, but before the first encore, I fought through the horde in an effort to make my way backstage. Feeling like a spawning salmon, I eventually managed to arrive at a door to the side of the stage, only to be stopped by a security guard the approximate size of a brick wall.

"Sorry," he said in a monotone voice. "No visitors."

Not to be deterred, I said in my most officious tone, "I'm Anna Christiansen, reporter from the *Gazette*, here to interview Rob Lazarus. He's expecting me."

"Sorry," he repeated. "No visitors." What was this guy, a robot? Little beads of sweat popped out on my forehead.

Up until now, I'd found that a camera and a clipboard gained you access almost anywhere. On the other hand, "anywhere" in my experience meant City Council meetings and store-ribbon cuttings.

I tried a half-hearted, "Let me talk to your supervisor," but knew the answer before the words left my mouth.

It's hard to think clearly when panic starts bubbling up like boiling oil. I gulped three deep breaths to tamp it down, forcing myself to focus. Options. What were my options? I could slink into work first thing in the morning and explain to Mr. K that a big bully with a three-word vocabulary had blocked my (career) path. That would be tantamount to kissing the future of my job goodbye. The thought made me want to throw up.

The guard raised an index finger, pointing toward the front of the theater and the exit. Dejected, I trudged in that direction, wondering where Rob Lazarus and his fellow rock stars were at that moment. Where were rock stars after any concert? Sneaking out the back door, trying to avoid the screaming hordes who'd just paid good money to see them. They'd have a limo or something waiting to whisk them away to their hotel or the bus station (Scandia was too small for an airport).

Eyeing the emergency-exit sign, its illumination fighting valiantly to break through a haze of decriminalized smoke, I decided to make my play. I'd wait them out in the alley behind the building. This wasn't as gutsy a move as you might think. With our almost nonexistent crime rate, my only risk was getting hit up for spare change by Mrs. Potter, Scandia's lone homeless person. If the band didn't leave via the rear exit, I'd be toast, especially because the door would lock behind me. But at least I had a plan. Better to go down swinging.

The night air was chillier than I'd anticipated; a fine mist clung close to the ground and I cursed myself for forgetting my sweater. Folding my arms around my body, I leaned against a surprisingly clean dumpster, keeping my eyes on the scarred metal door. So this was what real reporting was all about—hanging out in a back alley waiting to conduct an interview with a band that might already be long gone (something my J-school professors failed to mention).

The seconds dripped by in slow motion. I

checked my watch for the umpteenth time, shivered, and settled in for what could be a long fruitless wait. At what point would I give up and crawl home, defeated? That sounded like a decision best made through the filter of judgment and experience. Unfortunately, both were in short supply.

After last night's sleeplessness, I must have drifted into an uneasy slumber, because the sound of far-away laughter startled me into semi-awareness. Briefly disoriented to find I'd slumped into a sitting position, I struggled to my feet just as the door creaked open to reveal the Dickweeds in all their glory, lugging instrument cases and chattering away. I'd guessed right! Maybe I had the instincts of a reporter after all.

"Where the hell is the bus?" one of them asked. "I'm gonna kill Felix."

"Hope he remembered to make the motel reservations," said another.

"I'm so damned beat I could sleep right here," a third chimed in. "Wouldn't be the first time, that's for sure." With that, he looked right at me and said, "For you either, huh, miss?" He reached into his pocket and extracted a single dollar bill.

Ignoring the blush of embarrassment already sweeping across my face, I stammered, "Yes ... I mean no ... I mean, I wasn't sleeping, not exactly ... more like dozing. Uh ..." I stopped to see all five band members staring at me like I was some exotic monkey at the zoo. Too late to do anything now but soldier on with my well-rehearsed elevator speech. "I'm Anna Christiansen, reporter from the *Gazette*, here to interview Rob Lazarus."

"Looks like they don't pay reporters much around here, living in the alley and all."

That came from Lazarus himself, whom I recognized as the heart-throb leader of the band; his gorgeous face had appeared on all the posters around town and ads in the paper. I couldn't believe it, but he was even better-looking in person.

The flush deepened. "I don't live here. In the alley, I mean. I have a proper apartment, thank you very much. And my salary is none of your ..."

Thankfully, our so-called conversation was cut short by the wheeze of an ancient school bus squeezing into view, its yellow paint oxidized by years of neglect to a sick reddish brown.

"Well, boys, our ride's here," Lazarus said.

"Wait! Please. I just need a few minutes. For my story."

"Sorry, miss. Maybe next time."

There would, of course, be no next time. Not for little Scandia. And certainly not for me. So I did what any self-respecting journalist would do. I burst into tears. They gushed hot and bitter from a deep reservoir of frustration. The wracking sobs didn't help either. Or maybe they did.

"Geez, Rob, look what you made her do," said a guy in a knee-length black-leather coat who I sort of recognized as the bass player. "Give her five minutes. You're not big enough to be big-timing anybody just yet."

"Calling the shots now, Aaron? Telling me what to do? You give so much of a shit, you talk to her. I'm outta here." And with that, he disappeared into the bus.

The guy he called Aaron shrugged and threw me a sympathetic look. He wasn't as classically handsome as Lazarus, but something about him made my eyes go wide and my jaw flap open. Not only was he kind and considerate, but he looked just like Prince Charming in my favorite book of fairy tales (if Charming had been a vampire), right down to the jutting chin and long flowing locks. "Anywhere around here we can grab a cup of coffee at this hour?"

The tears screeched to a stop like someone had turned off the spigot. As a matter of fact, there was.

CHAPTER 4

"Here, wipe your eyes. Your mascara's running," Aaron said, handing me a Kleenex across the table.

I took it, inspected it briefly for any telltale former usage, and did as he suggested.

"Hey, I'm sorry about Rob," he continued. "I'll tell you a secret, as long as it's strictly off the record."

"Deal."

"The only girls he's ever nice to are the groupies. Obviously, you're not his type. A good thing, by the way."

The way he smiled at me, it almost looked like he was thinking that I was *his* type.

That was when Kim, our server, stopped by our booth, wearing an attitude and a button that said, "Sarcasm Served All Day." I sort of remembered her from high school, although our paths rarely crossed then (or now), and I doubted she knew what sarcasm meant.

The Grease Trap wasn't on my normal radar, situated on our version of the other side of the tracks. It mainly serviced truckers, cops, and folks just passing through. And reporters on deadline, apparently. I wondered if Kim had any recollection of me, or of high school, for that matter.

"Hi Anna," she said, barely looking at me at all. "Who's your friend?" She batted her eyes coyly.

"Hi, Kim. This is Aaron. Aaron, Kim."

She reached out a hand featuring nails accented by flaking remnants of purple polish. Aaron gave it a perfunctory shake.

"I don't think I've seen you in here before."

I cut her off. "Not to be rude, but can we order? I really need to get home before sunrise."

She recoiled. "That's a fine way to treat an old friend." Turning to Aaron again, she said, "Me and her went to high school together."

"Not English class," I said.

Kim missed my little joke, but Aaron grinned.

"Biology," she said. "Anna puked on dissection day. I swear she turned greener than that frog."

"Oh, for goodness sake!"

"Okay. Fine. Whatevs. What'll you have?" Directing the question at Aaron, as if I didn't exist.

He deferred to me.

"English muffin, dry," I said. "And hot tea."

"No frog's legs?" Her laugh was a wheeze.

"Just coffee for me," Aaron said.

"I'll be right back."

When she was out of earshot, I said, "And that's why I have to get out of this town someday."

Aaron chuckled and I noticed his dimples for the first time. They went well with the cleft in his chin. "You just broke the first rule of ordering."

"I know, I know. Never tick off your server."

"Better inspect that muffin carefully."

"Maybe I'll let you take the first bite."

His smile was crooked and fleeting. "No worries. I have a cast-iron stomach. You sort of have to when you live on the road."

I stared at him a second too long before forcing myself to focus on the business at hand. "Which is a perfect segue into my first question—"

"Here's your coffee!" Kim interrupted, gently setting a mug in front of Aaron. "Oh, and here's *your* order," she said to me. The cup was half the size of the mug and sported a crack to boot. And the muffin resembled a charcoal briquette. She favored me with a self-satisfied smirk before turning on her heels and sashaying over to the next table.

"Subtle, isn't she," Aaron said. "You were saying?"

"Right. Thank you for doing this. You really saved my butt."

"I could never resist a woman in distress. Besides, like I said, Rob can be a real asshole sometimes. I feel sort of obligated to prove we're not all jerks." That smile again. His soft brown eyes held mine and after my heart skipped a couple of beats, I finally had to turn away.

When I turned back, he was still gazing at me. Fumbling for my recorder, I asked, "Mind if I tape this?"

"Only if you promise not to blackmail me."

"Scout's honor. I was a Girl Scout for six whole months." I gave him the three-fingered scouting salute before hitting the record button. "Okay, here we go. I'm interviewing Aaron, uh, what's your last name?"

"Eisenberg."

"Help me with that."

He spelled it out.

"Aaron Eisenberg of the Dickweeds, an up-and-coming band from Las Vegas, Nevada. Almost famous, like in the movie. So what brings you to a town like Scandia?"

He took a thoughtful sip of coffee. "Well, we're definitely not famous. Not even *almost.* But we *are* popular."

I frowned. "I don't understand the distinction."

"To me, famous is when you walk down the street and hear someone humming your song. Or you get on an elevator and you're on the speakers. Or *The Enquirer* starts making up stories about you. We, on the other hand, have a fan base, small but loyal. I know a lot of them by name. We're getting bigger all the time, but we haven't broken through yet." He said this last part wistfully.

"Do you think you ever will?"

"On nights like this ..." he trailed off and shrugged.

I feverishly jotted down his thoughts. (I never totally trust the recorder.) After a couple of false starts, we were off and running.

"But why Scandia? You've played big cities, much larger venues. How'd you wind up here?"

"Ever read the book *Outliers?*"

Talk about an answer coming out of left field. I shook my head.

"The term comes from statistics. It means an observation that's distant from the rest of the data. The author uses the Beatles as an example. In their early years, they played all night every night in these little clubs in Hamburg, Germany, for like a year and a half. Tens of thousands of hours until they could do it in their sleep. Talk about distant from being the biggest band in the world. But when the opportunity came, they were ready."

"So this is your way of making sure you're ready?"

He brightened. "Exactly! We'll play anywhere, anytime. We've opened for the Killers, Imagine Dragons, War on Christmas, and Moondog Matinee. Headlined a blues festival in Lake Havasu, Arizona. Won our share of battles of the bands. But we've also played for tip money at dive bars and strip clubs and even a few bowling alleys. Oh, and a laundromat."

"A laundromat? Seriously?"

"Yep."

That smile again. My heart started pounding.

"As for Scandia, two nights ago, we had a gig in Grand Rapids. Our manager worked out the deal here at the last minute. We were just going home anyway. I have to say, the Royal's not a bad venue. A nice surprise, actually. And as you no doubt saw, even with two days' warning, we still brought out enough people to fill the place. Mostly."

"Well, we're proud of the Royal. How long has the band been together?"

He thought for a moment, twirling a strand of

mahogany shoulder-length hair around his index finger. "Depends on what you mean by 'together.' Officially, since college. It was on and off till our senior year when we got serious, because none of us had any job prospects."

"I know the feeling. Were you always the bass player? You're really good, by the way."

"Thank you, Anna. What did you say your last name was again?"

"Christiansen."

"Help me out with that."

Smiling at each other, I spelled it.

After a brief silence, he continued, "I've been slapping the bass ever since I heard Les Claypool on the radio when I was like eleven or twelve. That's not a euphemism, by the way. Although it could be, I suppose."

I grinned and he seemed happy that I got *his* little joke. A smart guy; how many people use "euphemism," not to mention references to statistics, in daily conversation?

"Claypool played bass for Primus. He was a real revelation; I had no idea you could do the kind of stuff he did. Bass players don't get much respect as a rule. We're largely invisible in our own band. But you'd definitely miss us if we weren't there. I'm not the greatest singer and I can't move like Jagger, so bass is perfect for me."

"Don't sell yourself short."

"You sound like my mom," he said. "I'm just being realistic. But she was a lounge singer back in the day, so she had a lot of opinions."

"That's what makes her a mom. Hey, wait a

minute. Did you say *had?* If you don't mind me asking ..."

Aaron shook his head slowly. "No, it's fine. She passed a few years back. Brain aneurysm. One second she's giving me a hard time and the next second, lights out. I still can't believe it sometimes."

"So it happened in front of you?"

"Uh-huh. I guess you never really get over it."

"I would think not. And your father?"

"Left when I was little. Never really knew him. Although I've seen pictures when he was younger and it's like looking at my own twin. I hope I didn't get his sense of responsibility. Or lack thereof. Genetics is a powerful thing."

"From what I've seen, you don't have to worry about that."

"That's nice of you to say."

"Just honest. So, you're an orphan. At what? Thirty?"

"Thirty-one."

"Well, this explains a lot."

"What do you mean?"

"May I get personal?"

Aaron chuckled softly. "I thought you already had. Sure, go ahead."

"Okay, well, here goes. You have this overwhelming sense of sadness pouring off you. At first I thought you were just serious, or even solemn, but it's more than that."

"No, it's not. What have you known me, like, an hour?"

"If that. Regardless, it's there. Trust me. Just

below the surface. Girls can sense these things."

He leaned forward, resting his head in his hands. "Sorry." Genuine, not petulant.

"Don't be. It's an appealing quality. I bet it's a chick magnet."

He considered this for a bit. "So, do you want to fix me?"

I peeked at the time and decided we needed to get our conversation back on track.

"Maybe later," I said, smiling to lighten the mood. "I'm on deadline."

"Okay, I'll take a raincheck."

Reviewing my notes to see where we left off, I said, "I'm sure you get this next question all the time, but I'm also sure my readers will want to know. What's with the name Dickweeds?"

"It means 'total losers.' Seemed appropriate at the time. Still might."

"I think I see a pattern developing."

Aaron shrugged. "What are you, a reporter or a psychologist?"

Before I could answer, Kim stopped by again to inquire about refills and annoy me further. "You might want to wrap this up," she said. "We close in ten minutes. Although *you're* welcome to stay," she said to Aaron. "We're having a little after-work birthday party for Curtis, one of the cooks."

"Sorry, I'm heading back to Las Vegas in the morning," he said. "But thanks for the invite." Her look of disappointment was palpable. Based on the pang in my stomach, mine was too.

After Kim disappeared into the kitchen, Aaron

said, “Actually, we’re not leaving until tomorrow afternoon.”

“You’re not? Great!” I said with too much exuberance. “I mean, uh, it’s late and you’ll want to get your sleep. I’m sure you have a long day ahead of you.”

“You still sound like my mom. Listen, believe it or not, I’m really enjoying this. It’s my first real interview. Usually, Rob hogs the spotlight. Want to continue back at the motel? No funny business, I promise.” He crossed his heart and hoped to die.

Another pang. The whole thing was just plain weird. Sure, I was between boyfriends. But I wasn’t the kind of girl who fell for someone after 45 minutes. At least not until now.

CHAPTER 5

A sliver of sunlight bled through a crack in the blackout shade, slicing through the darkness and illuminating the room just enough to reveal rumpled clothes strewn across the motel's lime-green carpet. Our clothes. My mouth tasted like the last swallow of coffee and my body felt like a toothache, no doubt a result of the broken-down mattress. Had it been a horse, they would have shot it by now.

I gently removed the left arm cradling my neck, slid noiselessly out of bed, and padded over to the bathroom, shutting the door softly. I had to pee, but more important, I had to think.

The previous evening had been one of many firsts. My first real assignment. My first interview with someone more famous (okay, popular) than the mayor's wife. And my first one-night stand.

How did I feel about that exactly? Not cheap and used, like I thought I might (if I'd stopped beforehand to consider it at all). Actually, it was exhilarating. It had seemed like the most natural thing in the world. It still did. None of my other experiences (and there weren't that many) had left me so ... what? Light. Joyful. No, joyous.

I'd never believed in a soulmate. My friends talked about it, books and movies revolved around it, songs seeped it from the radio. But so far, it had passed me by. I was always on the outside looking in. The funny thing was, I had plenty of company at the window, all of us with our noses pressed up against the glass. Enough to make me think the concept was some unattainable ideal invented to keep hope alive. Sure, you could fall madly in love. But the idea that you were destined to cross paths with The One, out of all the humans on the planet, just didn't make sense. Until now.

Now I understood that sense and logic had nothing to do with it. This took place on a purely emotional level, which happened to be somewhat foreign territory for me. Yet here it was. I felt like Aaron and I had known each other our entire lives. Just thinking his name made my heart soar.

When we had arrived back at the Michigander Motel (home of the free continental breakfast and a coveted one-star auto-club rating, according to the plastic plaque on the wall), spending the night there had been the last thing on my mind. Well, maybe not the last thing, but it certainly didn't occupy a top spot on my to-do list. However, the rest of the interview had flowed so effortlessly, and had become so personal, it might have been inevitable.

The room consisted of a queen-size bed, a rickety nightstand, a small round table with two mismatched chairs, and a green threadbare sofa that sort of matched the shag carpet. And the telltale stench of cigarettes despite the "No Smoking" sign. After testing out the chairs and deeming them unacceptable, we moved to the sofa, our knees so close to touching it felt like a bridge of chain lightning arcing between us. Trying my best to ignore it, I fired up the recorder and readied myself for round two.

"You mentioned you need to be back in Las Vegas. How come?"

"We have a meeting with a rep from Maiden America Records," he said without much enthusiasm.

I had enough for both of us. "Really? That's awesome!"

Aaron shrugged. "Not exactly. We've been down this road too many times, so close we could taste it. Even inked a deal once with a smaller company. But the first thing they wanted to do was change everything about us. Our look, our songs, our sound. Why do people do that? Made us all wonder why they were so hot for us in the first place."

"The thrill of the chase?" I offered.

"Who knows? So I try not to get too up or too down until there's a reason. Besides, this could be our last chance. Or mine, at any rate."

"What do you mean?" I asked, surprised.

"I'm thirty-one; thirty-two in August. That's how long I've given myself to be successful in this business."

"Seems kind of arbitrary, if you ask me."

"Not really. Ten years. Hard to believe it's been that long since we all graduated and made a run at it. But did you ever see that movie *Bull Durham*?"

"No."

"Kevin Costner plays a baseball player who's knocked around on farm teams for twelve years. He sets a minor-league record for the most career home runs, but he only makes it to the majors for twenty-one days."

"So that's how you see yourself?"

"That's how I don't want to see myself. Nothing sadder than some has-been or never-was desperately hanging on for one more shot. I've run into a lot of that type. The whole scene's changing and they don't see it. This is a young person's game. Well, that's not me. I'll cut my hair and get a real job before I turn into a cartoon. You gotta grow up some time, right? Childish things and all that."

All I could think of to say was, "Don't cut your hair!" What an idiot I was. I felt my cheeks grow hotter by the second.

He looked at me quizzically and smiled that smile. "Okay, I'll think about it. Depends on the job, I suppose."

Time to get back to professionalism. "What will you do? What else are you good at?"

He leaned back and stretched his long legs. "I sold cars for a while. Volvos. Made a decent living. The old ladies loved me."

Not just the old ones, I thought. And worried he could read my mind.

"I'm also a pretty good audio engineer," he continued. "But those gigs are few and far between. With today's technology, bands are doing it themselves. That's another reason the labels are dying—except for Maiden and a handful of others that seem to know what they're doing. I hear they're trying to pump up their American rosters, which means there's a glimmer of hope. We're American, after all. Last I checked."

"Well, let's hope it doesn't come to that. Getting a job, I mean. I have a good feeling about your meeting."

"Yeah? How's your track record with those feelings?"

"Actually, not so great," I had to admit. "But there's a first time for everything." I was living proof of that.

Staring out the window into the glare of the parking-lot lights, he said, "We could get lucky. I think about luck a lot. When we first started out, I thought success was inevitable. If you had talent and worked hard, somebody would notice. You know, the cream rises to the top."

"I believe that, too."

"Not me; not anymore. I've seen too many amazing bands fall by the wayside, bands that deserved to be successful. As good, if not better, than the ones you hear on the radio. The only difference, far as I can tell, is that some guys caught a break and some didn't." He slumped back into the couch with a defeated sigh.

"Well, that's depressing," I said.

"Tell me about it. I usually don't talk like this, unless I'm exhausted. That's when my guard comes down. And now I'm spilling my guts to a reporter. Rob and the guys are gonna kill me."

"Want me to leave it off the record? This isn't '60 Minutes,' you know. I'm not trying to ambush anyone here."

He thought for a moment. "Nah, keep it in. If this is gonna be my first and last interview, I want it to be real. Funny, you have a way of making me feel so comfortable. I've never said half this stuff out loud before. To anyone. It's mostly dark thoughts that creep up on you in the middle of the night. I hope it doesn't come off as whining. Or sour grapes."

"No, just honest. But my offer still stands."

He shook his head. "Let the chips fall. That's a Vegas term."

"Okay, but promise me one thing." I leaned forward, took his hands in mine, and stared into his eyes, thereby breaking one of the cardinal rules of journalism. (Something about objectivity. At that instant, I couldn't remember the others, either.) If my move caught him by surprise (it certainly caught me), he didn't show it.

"Anything."

"Please, please, please don't quit. Not just yet anyway, no matter what happens with Maiden. The band's too good. You're too good. It would be such a waste. And you'll regret it." The moisture on my cheek came as a shock to me, the second time that night Aaron had seen me cry. "I don't know what's gotten into me," I said. "I'm not a crier, honest."

In response, he wiped away my tear with his thumb. And followed it with a kiss, soft and gentle. With that simple gesture, I felt my mind, body, and soul open up to him completely.

I thought I'd made love before this night. But I was wrong.

❧O☙

And now it was the morning after, and here I was, sitting on the toilet in a cheap motel room, my legs getting more numb by the second. With no clue what was going to happen next. And then a disturbing thought. What if this was different for Aaron? Maybe he hooked up with a local girl in every town he played. I could be just another in a long line of conquests getting ready to do the walk of shame. I shuddered, stood up, flushed, fluffed my hair without looking in the mirror, opened the door, and stepped back into the room with all the confidence of a bunny rabbit. Outside in the parking lot, the sounds of car doors slamming and trash cans clanging intruded on our low-rent haven, signaling the start of a new day.

"Good morning," Aaron said. He was still in bed, leaning up on one elbow. Instinctively, I tried to cover my unbuttoned shirt with both arms. "Don't," he said. "You're beautiful."

"I'm not."

"You have no idea. That's one of the things I like most about you. I could look at you every day for the rest of my life."

Did he say "for the rest of my life?" I took his outstretched hand and slipped back under the covers.

"You're trembling," he said as he folded me in his embrace. "Cold?"

"Scared. Scared last night wasn't real. Scared I'll never see you again."

His gaze was earnest. He put his finger to my

lips and quelled my fears with three simple words. "Come with me."

Words I longed to hear and dreaded just the same. The trembling stopped and relief washed over me a nanosecond before logic took over. "I want to. More than anything. But I can't. Not now. I have my work, family, responsibilities, people who depend on me. But soon. Let me tie up some loose ends and I'll meet you, say, in a month?"

"You won't," he said. Before I could fire back in hurt or anger, he followed with an explanation. "Back when I sold cars, we had a word for customers who said they were close to buying, but needed to think it over. 'Be-backs.' As in, 'I'll be back tomorrow.' Know how many actually did? None. Not a single solitary one. That's because they let somebody—a wife, husband, friend, whoever—talk them out of it. Or they talked themselves out of it. Because the brain always operates out of fear."

Mine sure did. Was it just the used-car guy, trying to make a sale? Or was it ... something more?

"You need to follow your heart. If you don't do it now, you never will."

His words cut deep and my trembling picked up where it had left off. Pulling me in even closer, he kissed me gently, then not so gently.

"Do you promise? Not to leave me flat, dump me in the middle of the desert, make me sneak back to Scandia with my tail tucked?"

"I do."

"Okay." I heard myself gasp. "Let's do it."

CHAPTER 6

"Mom, Dad, I'm not asking permission. I'm telling you my plans." There, I said it. And thought I might pass out. My voice was not my voice; it was more like watching a movie starring me. With no guarantee of a happily ever after.

My mother's face, devoid of color, her mouth working to form words that wouldn't come. My father, expression set like Mount Rushmore, a knot of muscle protruding from the place where his jaw joined his skull. And Aaron, standing next to me, arms folded in protective mode, no doubt wishing he played no role at all in our little family soap opera.

We were still in the foyer of my parent's home, the house I grew up in, whose familiar country furnishings and knick-knacks (my mother collected bells everywhere she went—only she knew why) still possessed the power to comfort and repel me at the same time. We never made it into the living room, because I couldn't stop myself from blurting out, "This is Aaron. I'm moving to Las Vegas with him," the moment I walked in the door. It was that or faint or vomit all over the rooster area rug we'd had my entire life. (My mother loved that rug, even though the rooster was getting a little long in the beak. She called it a "collector's item," to which my father always harrumphed, "Yeah, garbage collectors.")

So this was my fault; I had no allusions otherwise. I owned the moment. I suppose I could have handled the announcement more delicately, but this was my first time moving across country with a boy I'd just met. Where's the AP Stylebook for something like that?

After more lip and mouth gyrations that might have looked comical under different circumstances, my mother sputtered, "Peter, talk some sense into her. She can't do this, can she?" At that moment, she looked so small and vulnerable, I resisted the impulse to wrap my arms around her. That wouldn't have helped my cause one iota.

At length, my father, his jaw muscle relaxing slightly, replied, "Sure she can, Mama." He'd always been a hard man to read, hiding behind that superhuman Nordic restraint that must have skipped a generation, bypassing me entirely. But it seemed like he was softening a little.

My mother turned to me with the saddest eyes and said, "But why, Anna? This isn't like you."

I swallowed hard and said, "I've lived my entire life doing things that are like me and look where it's gotten me. Nowhere."

"Your life is so bad?"

And now the tears came. I stood there frozen, biting my lip to keep from telling her, I don't mean it; it's all a big misunderstanding. Instead, I plowed ahead while I still had some resolve in the tank.

"Not bad. Just boring. And predictable. I'm almost twenty-five. If I don't get out of here now, I never will!" My left eye started twitching like crazy and I prayed nobody would notice.

"But your career?"

"Mom, it's not a career, just a job. A dead-end one at that. What's the best I can hope for? Copy editor in five years? Who knows if the paper will even be around by then? I want more! Didn't you ever want more? Wanna be more?" Fear giving way to defiance. To my parents, I'm sure it looked like a tantrum, a five-year-old stomping her little foot. Were they going to send me to my room next? It probably hadn't occurred to them I didn't live with them anymore.

My mother, between sniffs, said, "But why Las Vegas? And why this boy?" She pointed at him like a victim picking out a suspect in a lineup.

Aaron, bless his heart, stepped forward and said, "Aaron, ma'am. My name is Aaron Eisenberg. And I'm not a boy. I'm thirty-one years old." He stuck out his hand (trembling ever so slightly) and my mother shook it reluctantly, as if he were holding a jellyfish.

"Of course," she conceded. "Aaron. I'm sorry. You have a name." She turned to me. "Why Aaron?" Making a point of it.

I couldn't think of a logical explanation, so I settled on the truth. "I love him, Mom."

That's when my father's face went all five-alarm. He was slow to boil, but when he did, look out. "Love!" If he'd been a cartoon character, steam would have come billowing out of his ears. I jumped despite myself. His anger always had that effect on me, even though he never did more than bellow. "Love! You just met the lad." (My father calls every male under thirty-five a "lad.") "It's not real. Couldn't be. Have you lost your mind?"

I couldn't deny the possibility. But I rallied nonetheless. "Maybe. But let me ask you. When did you know you were in love with Mom?"

He narrowed his eyes and shook his head back and forth like an old lion. "Not after twelve hours, certainly."

Awkward silence as I looked to my mother for any sign of support. The Minnesota Vikings' cuckoo clock in the kitchen marked the seconds. Even though we live in Michigan, my parents are devout Vikings fans. More of that Nordic thing, no doubt.

At last it came. "I knew," she said in a voice both quiet and steely.

My father raised an eyebrow as we all stared in his direction. "Knew what, Mother?"

"Knew I was in love the moment I laid eyes on you at the freshman dance. Although for the life of me, I can't remember why."

"Impossible!" The god of thunder in retreat.

She jabbed a finger into his lumberjack chest. "Don't you tell me what I felt, Peter Christiansen."

"See? See?" I jumped in, a defense attorney fighting for my own life, awash in the glow of my mother's remembrance.

He stopped backing up and held his ground.

"Irrelevant. A different time. Simpler. The world is a much more dangerous place. How do we know this, this, Aaron isn't some kind of serial killer?"

Aaron matched his gaze. "Ask me anything, sir."

I wanted to kiss him. Okay, I always wanted to kiss him. But now I really wanted to.

Time for the third degree. My father was very good at the third degree. He had a lot of practice with previous boyfriends, all of whom cracked under the pressure. Of course, they were 16 and 17 at the time, so they didn't have a lot of experience. And the stakes were lower. As much as it made me want to hide in a closet, part of me was dying to find out what Aaron was made of.

"All right," my father said, cracking a knuckle and fixing Aaron with his patented laser beam stare. "What do you do for a living?"

Aaron stared right back. "I'm a bass player. In a band."

My father snorted, waving a calloused hand dismissively. "That's not a job! It's a hobby!"

"Sir, with all due respect, we work all the time. We're quite popular."

But not famous, I thought, stifling a smile. Already we shared an inside joke. A real "Breakfast at Tiffany's" moment, according to the old song. If that wasn't a solid foundation to build on, I didn't know what was.

"How much did you make last year?"

"Forty-three thousand."

Really? As a bass player? Wow. Almost double what I made. I was impressed.

"Chump change." He looked to my mother for confirmation, but there was none coming.

"I know it doesn't sound like much," Aaron said, "but we have a meeting next week with a big record company and ..."

My father cut him off. "When I was your age, I made ..."

My mother cut him off. "A lot less."

"Holy hell, Margaret! Whose side are you on?"

"No sides. I want the same thing you do, for our daughter to be safe. And happy. But we also need to 'keep it real,' as the kids say."

I didn't have the heart to tell her the kids don't say that anymore.

"But adjusting for inflation ..." he trailed off, knowing he'd already lost this round. After a brief pause, he changed tacks. "What kind of name is that anyway? Eisenstein?"

"Berg," Aaron corrected. "Eisenberg. It's German."

Uh-oh, I thought. My father hated the Germans. He never really talked about it much, but I could tell by the way he glowered at the TV when he watched old World War II movies. I think he lost some family members when the Germans invaded Norway, something he made me watch with him on the History Channel.

I heard Aaron take a deep breath. "And Jewish."

My father tilted his head in thought. We were Lutheran, but only during the holidays. I had no idea how he felt about Jewish people. I had no idea how I felt either. We didn't know any. This was certainly news to me. And heading in an unexpected direction.

"Orthodox? Conservative? Reform? Reconstruction? By your appearance, I assume you're not Hasidic."

His questions surprised me. I guessed those were religious branches or something, although he might as well have been speaking a foreign language. Maybe there was more to the man than I ever imagined.

"My parents were Conservative, but I'm not observant. Just ethnic."

My father ran his fingers through his graying blonde hair and said, "I see." I didn't, but I could always ask Aaron later. "Okay," he continued. "Write down three references for me. No relatives. I'm going to call them. And google you." He turned in my direction. "And then your mother and I will discuss this in private. Stay put. We can't stop you from leaving, Anna; I know that. But we can withhold our blessing."

With that, he strode out of the foyer and into his study. My mother hurried over to me and gave me a quick reassuring hug before following suit. The study door clicked shut.

"Now what?" Aaron asked. "Can we sit?"

"Probably a good idea," I said, motioning to our company couch in the living room.

We could be in for a long wait.

CHAPTER 7

Stuck somewhere in the shadowlands between melancholy and elation, I opted for the latter. "Woo-hoo!" I whooped, throwing my arms around Aaron as he drove through our development. Despite the lingering gloom, I knew the door to my new life stood wide open, just waiting for me to crash through. I hadn't felt this free since, well, ever. Not even my college graduation compared to this.

"Hey!" he feigned annoyance. "You're gonna get us killed."

"Not likely. The only people who drive here anymore are my folks. Everyone else is too old."

Aaron planted a big wet kiss on my lips before shifting the Ford into third and focusing his attention on the road. "That was intense."

"You'll get tired of kissing me eventually," I joked. "Like when I'm ninety."

He grinned. "No, I mean that whole scene. I felt like a defendant waiting for the jury to come back and deliver their verdict."

"That's just my father's way. I've been dealing

with it my whole life. Doesn't make it any easier, though."

"So did you have a clue?"

"Sort of. I could see that my father began to accept the inevitable right away. And my mother was actually leaning in our direction and she has a lot of pull. She's the only person in the world he's afraid of."

A point in our favor. We'd been waiting on the couch for more than an hour, too scared to get a drink or even go to the bathroom for fear of missing their re-entrance. We could hear muffled voices through the door (at least no yelling, as far as we could tell), but couldn't make out the words. Just when I thought I'd used up my last ounce of patience, the door opened with a series of squeaks, a noise my father had been promising to repair ever since my kindergarten days. Aaron and I sprung up like jack-in-the-boxes and dashed back to the foyer.

I couldn't read either of their expressions. A quick glance at Aaron told me he was more in the dark than I was. Our eyes darted back and forth between one and the other until, at last, my mother slipped me the tiniest of half-smiles. I exhaled, only then realizing I'd been holding my breath.

"Your father has something to tell you," she said.

He stood there frozen for a moment before clearing his throat. "Your mother and I have discussed the matter and I ..."

"We," she corrected. "We have decided to give you our blessing."

Aaron reached for my hand that was already waiting for him, giving it a reassuring squeeze. Both of us instinctively knew that a showy display of emotion would be out of place at this moment. I also knew my father was just getting warmed up.

"That's not entirely accurate," he said, giving my mother a sideward glance to make sure he wasn't upsetting her. "Your mother is giving you her blessing. Mine is more, um, conditional."

Which is when he laid out the whole ball of strings attached. I was to call home once a week, email at least once a day, and post all important photos on Facebook. Also, file my final story, because I didn't want to burn any bridges (in my father's world, burning bridges was one of the worst sins you could commit) and I'd need a good recommendation to get a new job, don't pick up hitchhikers (they were all psycho killers who had just escaped from maximum-security mental institutions), and use sun block. There were more, but by then I had tuned out.

"Questions?" he asked finally, making it sound like an ultimatum. When we had none, he said, "Mother?"

"Not a question, exactly," she said, her eyes glistening. "Just this. I remember the day you were born like it was yesterday. From that point in my life, everything changed. At the time, I couldn't possibly understand the depth of my feelings for you, the kind of love that overpowers everything else. And it's just grown stronger. Other than that first day when I put you on the bus for kindergarten, this is the hardest thing I've ever had to do." She paused to dab at her eyes with the bottom of her apron. "But you're an adult woman with your own life to live, your own dreams to follow. I'm not going to stand in your way. It's time I let go and trust that your father and I raised you right and you'll always remember the lessons we taught you." She tried to say more, but her voice cracked and she just stood there looking like Eeyore and for the second time that morning, I felt like forgetting the whole idea and moving back into my bedroom for all eternity. But I knew it was a trap; if I gave in and took the easy way out, it would eventually become a prison from which there would be no escape and I'd be just like my cousin June in Cheboygan, who ran from every opportunity and was now in danger of fading away completely. Instead, I just gave her a final hug that would have to hold us both until the next time we were together.

"I suppose you're going then," my father interrupted, shifting his weight from one foot to the other.

I let go of my mother and nodded.

"Very well," he said and reached in his back pocket for his wallet. Extracting a large wad of cash, he offered it to Aaron.

"Thank you, sir, but no. I have more than enough to get us home."

Home. The word jarred me in unexpected ways.

My father made one last lukewarm attempt at convincing Aaron to take the money before returning it to his pocket. "Well, that's, uh, good," he said. Was this another of his little tests? If so, Aaron passed with flying colors.

"We'll be fine, Daddy," I said, realizing I hadn't called him that since I was a little girl. If it occurred to him, he didn't let on. But my mother and I exchanged a knowing look.

More hugs, more stalling, before we found ourselves on the front porch. There, my father placed a hand on Aaron's shoulder and squeezed. His pit-bull grip elicited a wince, but Aaron stood his ground and took it without so much as a flinch. A closing test, perhaps? And a clear message. If you harm my daughter in any way, you'll get a lot more than this.

As we backed out of the driveway, I stuck my head out the car window and waved and watched my parents wave back until they grew smaller and smaller, disappearing entirely when Aaron turned the corner with a farewell beep of the horn.

CHAPTER 8

I suppose I always knew, at some level, I wouldn't be staying. Maybe that's why I lived like a transient; no pets, no plants, not even a picture on the wall of my furnished apartment. And, oh yeah, no friends to speak of. They'd all fled long before me and rarely returned.

So when we swung by my place to collect my stuff, it took all of 15 minutes to pack, after the hour I spent composing my Dickweeds story and emailing it to Mr. Knudsen, at the end of which, I added a personal note: "This will be my last story for the *Scandia Gazette*. Thank you for everything. I have decided to pursue an opportunity out of state."

Clothes, a few books and DVDs, some jewelry and toiletries, a keepsake or two, my laptop, a little cash, my favorite pillow, not much else. Except for the computer and money, it all fit in a large pink Little Mermaid suitcase, a souvenir of our trip to Disney World when I was nine. (Aaron, to his credit, didn't say a word about it, although he might have done a double take.)

I dashed off a brief note to Mrs. Fisker, my landlady (she was going to be pissed), left my key on the countertop, and walked out the front door without so much as a backward glance. It snapped shut with a satisfying click.

"You okay?" Aaron asked.

"Better than okay," I said with a reassuring smile. "But we need to make one more stop on our way out of town."

"No problem. Where we going?"

"Auntie's house."

I had seven aunts and uncles, but only one Auntie. "Auntie" is an exalted title seldom earned and rarely bestowed. It signifies that the recipient is a best friend, trusted confidante, and a bit of a character. Auntie was three for three. She was my mother's half-sister (same father), 14 years her elder, and the most flamboyant person in the little town where they'd both lived their whole lives. Auntie and my mother couldn't be more different. Whereas my mother was quiet, conservative, and seldom left Scandia, Auntie was loud, free-spirited, and probably stepped foot on every continent except Antarctica. (And I'm not so sure about that one.) When I was little, I found myself wishing she were my mother, that maybe there was a mix-up at the hospital. I loved her dearly, trusted her completely, and couldn't imagine leaving without a lemonade and a hug.

Auntie's house was a two-story faded-yellow Victorian badly in need of a new coat of paint. It sat on an oversized lot on the outskirts of Scandia, surrounded by a vibrant jungle of foliage that looked like it was planted by a kindergarten class wielding sacks of random seeds. Rose bushes, apple and dogwood trees, honeysuckles and hollies all seemed to be vying for the same turf in an atmosphere of peaceful, if not playful, coexistence. As Aaron and I stepped through the picket-fence gate (it gave way with a despondent groan), I found myself thinking, as I always did, that a machete would not be out of the question. Auntie, of course, would have none of that. The surroundings, like the house itself, were a physical extension of her unique style and suited her just fine.

Before we could bound up the rickety porch steps (seven of them to be exact; I counted them every time I went up and down as a girl), the front door swung open and there she stood, a welcoming smile on her face. She wore one of the trademark designer floral-print dresses she'd brought back from Paris before I was born, the black and red one I remembered as a child, now faded and frayed and showing its age. She must have known something was up. When we hugged, she held on a few seconds longer than usual.

"Child, I've been expecting you," she said in her alto voice, strong as ever, confirming my suspicion that Mother had tipped her off. Turning to Aaron, she said, "And this, obviously, is your young man. Aren't you going to introduce us?"

Before I could say a word, she offered her hand like she was ready for it to be kissed. Aaron, to my surprise, did just that.

"Of course, Auntie. This is Aaron Eisenberg. Aaron, the one and only Auntie Dort."

"Short for Dorothy. It's Anna's fault, if you must know. She could never pronounce my name as a young girl."

"It suits you, I think," Aaron said, and Auntie favored him with a smile.

"So you're a member of the tribe," she said.

Aaron frowned in confusion. "I beg your pardon?"

"The Hebrew tribe." Before Aaron could take offense, she continued, "Lucky for you two. It sealed the deal for your father."

"What do you mean?" I asked, excited that our small mystery was about to be solved.

"You know he was in Desert Storm, right?"

"Yes, but he never talks about it. I wish he would sometimes."

"Well, what you don't know is he almost died there. One of those homemade explosive thingies blew up only a few feet away from him. Another soldier, his best friend, stepped in front of it and took the full force of the blast. He died instantly, of course. Your father caught some shrapnel in his shoulder and leg, but it could have been so much worse. The soldier's name was Alan Bernstein."

"A Jew," Aaron said.

Auntie nodded. "So now you understand." She shivered before adding, "Let's get off this porch. There's a bit of a chill in the air."

I didn't feel it in the air, but I had goose bumps all over from the story of my father and the explosion and his friend's sacrifice. It explained so many things about him—and I wished I'd known about it, that someone had told me before the minute I was leaving our home to start a new life. That he'd been so unexpectedly familiar with the branches of the Jewish religion also suddenly made sense.

We followed Auntie through the screen door, past the entry hall with every inch of wall space covered by collector's plates accumulated during her world travels, and into the parlor where a pitcher of fresh-squeezed lemonade and plate of Frisbee-sized oatmeal cookies awaited. The cozy sitting room, like the rest of the house, smelled of lavender and mothballs. (Come to think of it, so did Auntie.) The aroma transported me back to my childhood faster than any time machine, and I envisioned myself on this same floor, playing dress-up with Heidi, the world's most patient collie, somehow managing to maintain her dignity while wearing a blue-and-white milk-maid's bonnet. If I squinted just enough, I could picture Uncle Joe sitting in his recliner, an unlit pipe in his mouth and a newspaper in his hands, occasionally peering over the top of his glasses to make sure the dog and I were still on good terms.

After settling into the white high-back chairs that had obviously been purchased at two different second-hand stores at two different times, Auntie's voice snapped us back to the here and now.

"Your parents are very ..." she paused to choose her words carefully, "concerned." Getting right to the point in true Auntie fashion.

"They shouldn't be," I said, sounding more annoyed than I'd planned.

She leaned forward. "I'll let you in on a little secret. No matter how old you get, your parents will always see you as a little girl. Their little girl. The good news is, they didn't ask me to talk you out of it."

I reached for Aaron's hand and found it waiting for me. I had worried they'd change their minds the minute I left the house.

Auntie cleared her throat and took a sip of lemonade, glancing at Aaron and back to me before saying, "And you know I wouldn't, even if I could."

Those were the words I needed to hear, the ones that showed Auntie was still on my side. I choked back a sob. "Why wouldn't you, Auntie?" Not sounding like a grown woman at all.

"I'm going to tell you a story, one you've never heard before."

I loved Auntie's stories and the thought of a new one made me sit up straighter in my chair.

"When I was a young lady of seventeen, I met a boy, Donald Ellis. Donnie. I was living in this very house with my parents, your grandfather and my stepmother, your mom's mom. Your mother was around three. Donnie came for the summer to stay with his cousins across the street, a city boy up from Detroit for some fresh air and maybe to get away from a bit of trouble. I can still picture him there, chopping wood, a strapping young man with a mop of dirty blond hair and a big toothy grin. We became inseparable. Movies—we still had the drive-in back then over on old Orchard Road—ice cream, the lake. The days flew by and before I knew it, it was time for him to go home. He begged me to go with him, but I was starting college in Kalamazoo in the fall and it wasn't meant to be. The day he left was the saddest of my life, like a little death. The hurt in my stomach was like nothing I'd ever felt."

She paused to take another swallow of lemonade and when she resumed her tale, her eyes were moist. Although she looked right at us, I could tell her mind was 50 years away. I could also tell that Aaron was as enthralled as I was.

"So what happened, Auntie?"

"We wrote. But the letters became fewer and fewer as time passed. And one day they just stopped. Years later, I heard he'd served in Vietnam, came home, got married, opened a small chain of furniture stores out west. By then, I'd met your Uncle Joe. We were married forty-two years, until the stroke."

Auntie paused again and Aaron and I shared a look, not sure what to make of her story. We sat in silence for a few moments, listening to the muffled trill of crickets filtering in from the garden. As if reading our minds, she said, "The point is, I've thought of Donnie every day since. Every single day. He was the love of my life."

I'm sure my expression betrayed my surprise. "But what about Uncle Joe?"

"I loved him too, of course. But different. We were comfortable from the beginning, like a couple of old sweaters. Maybe it was better this way."

Aaron's turn to chime in. "How so?"

"The kind of love Donnie and I felt, I don't know if you can sustain it. We might have burnt out."

She paused for a beat. "But oh, what a glorious fire!"

Auntie settled back in her chair with a sigh and it sounded like the ancient house answered in agreement. Ordinarily, I might have been embarrassed for her, as I usually was when old people talked about love and passion. But all I felt was sadness.

Aaron felt it too. "That's a bittersweet story, ma'am."

Bittersweet. A songwriter's word. I fell in love with him all over again.

"Young man," Auntie said. "Sometimes bittersweet is the best we can hope for." She cast her eyes on me again and now her voice had that old resolve. "But not for you, Anna. You and Aaron deserve better. So you go to that Las Vegas and live your lives. No regrets, you hear me? Your parents will be just fine. I'll be just fine."

Tears of relief filled my eyes and, for the first time, I realized how badly I wanted—no, needed—someone's unconditional permission. And the fact that it came from Auntie made it even better. We stood and I threw my arms around her. "I love you, Auntie."

"I love you more. Promise me you'll call your parents at least once a week like they asked and let them know you're fine."

I held up my right hand. "Solemnly swear. I'll call you, too."

"Save your money and drop me a line on Facebook. You've got better things to do than waste your time talking to an old woman."

"Oh, Auntie, you're not old." I chuckled to myself. My mother was old. Auntie was ancient.

As we walked arm in arm to the front door, I gave her one final squeeze. She brushed a stray strand of hair from my face before turning her attention to Aaron.

"Take good care of my niece," she said, "or you'll have me to deal with."

CHAPTER 9

"'White Room.' Jefferson Airplane."

Aaron frowned. "Good one. How could you possibly know that?"

"My mom. You'd never guess to look at her, but she's a classic rocker. Back in the day before they were classics. I grew up listening to Cream, Zeppelin, the Doors, Creedence. Especially Creedence. She'd blast those vinyl records from our old Kenwood system so she could hear them while she vacuumed. She cherished that stereo; I wasn't even allowed to touch it until I was sixteen. I remember that being a bigger deal than when I got my driver's license."

I peered out the window at the seemingly endless patchwork of farmland checker-boarding the landscape, indicating we were still somewhere in the Midwest. Already, I was farther from my home than I'd ever been on my own and my giddy exhilaration showed no signs of tapering off, like the way you feel on the first day of summer vacation. I loved the idea that not a soul in the world knew where we were at this particular moment. I had a feeling it might not ever happen again. As if to validate my thoughts, a billboard featuring a smiling cow touting something called "Future Hay" whizzed past, making me wonder how they could possibly improve on the original. Some kind of GMO thing, perhaps? Ahead, a straight ribbon of highway lay before us, an unbroken promise unspooling toward the horizon.

"It's your turn," I reminded Aaron.

"Wow, you're in an awfully big hurry to lose. Okay, 'Back in Black,' AC/DC. Bam!" He let out what sounded like a satisfied whoop.

"Oh please. 'Knights in White Satin.'" Fast, giving him no time to think. I, on the other hand, had four more titles in the queue. "Moody Blues."

Instead of another song, Aaron responded in a passable British accent: "Breathe deep the gathering gloom. Watch lights fade from every room."

"Show-off. You don't get extra points for lyrics, you know."

"Just proving that two can play this game. I was in a sixties' cover band for like a week and a half."

"When?"

"Oh, a few years ago, when Lazarus decided he wanted to try to go solo. It was actually for around three months—and I even got to sing a few tunes. 'Knights in White Satin' was one of them."

"That song used to scare the crap out of me when I was little. Sometimes my father would work late and my mother would fall asleep with the radio on. And that voice would drift in from the other room and wake me up and I'd lie there shaking, too afraid to go back to sleep, thinking thoughts no six-year-old should ever think ..."

"Now who's stalling," Aaron said.

"You're such a brat," I said, punching him playfully in the arm. "I'm pouring my heart out and all you care about is winning some stupid game. Besides, it's still your turn."

"Oh, right. 'Black Balloon.' Goo Goo Dolls. Let's at least bring it into the modern era. No way I'm losing this tiebreaker to you."

We'd been going at it since Davenport. Aaron had kicked my butt in the "Sun and Rain" and "Transportation" categories (who knew 409 was a car engine? I made him google it before conceding), while I cleaned up in "Animals" and "Girl's Names." And here we were, locked in mortal combat in the all-important "Black and White" finale with dinner on the line. My brain was beginning to feel like oatmeal.

"Go already," he said.

"Fine. 'White Christmas.' By like a million different artists."

"Name one."

I started to sweat. I could see the guy's face. My parents watched that old movie every December. "Crap!"

Aaron slapped the steering wheel with his right hand and began whistling the Final Jeopardy theme, in perfect pitch no less. I could feel the game, my free dinner, and my bragging rights slipping away by the note. In desperation, I silently recited the alphabet, hoping the right letter would trigger a flicker of memory. On the second go-around, I stubbed my brain on "C."

"Crosby!" I blurted out just as the final tone faded.

"First name. The judges need both names."

Luckily, it clicked into place effortlessly. "Bling!" I'm not sure, but I may have smirked.

"Ha! You lose."

"What? No way." My face felt sunburned.

"Way. It's Bing. That's dinner's gonna be extra delish; free food always tastes better."

In response, I fished around in my purse for my pen and reporter's spiral notepad, making two notations.

Aaron turned toward me. "What are you doing?"

"Just jotting down a few notes. Demerits, actually. You're a bad winner. And you said 'delish.' I can't possibly be with a man who says 'delish.' You can turn around at the next exit."

Panic washed over Aaron's face, which made my heart hurt. "Just kidding, you big idiot," I said, finally. I should have tortured him a few moments longer, but couldn't bring myself to do it. His look of relief was all the confirmation I needed. Apparently, 18 hours, give or take, wasn't enough time to establish the necessary trust to joke around like that—although I was still semi-serious about "delish." Loosening my seat belt, I slid closer to him and rested my head on his shoulder. "I could never leave you for something like that," I said. "Unless we were close to an airport."

He gave me a little push and I returned to my

previous position. “Fine,” he said, sticking out that full lower lip.

“Fine,” I said.

We continued in silence for a few minutes before Aaron said, “Wanna hear something cool about ‘White Christmas’?”

“Sure. I don’t have anything better to do. Now that I’m staying and all.”

“It was written by a Jewish guy. Irving Berlin. How ironic is that? The number-one Christmas song of all time was written by a member, as Auntie says, of the tribe.”

“And that matters why?”

“Well, let’s just say Jews like it when one of our own makes good. Especially when we get over on the Christians.”

“What do you have against Christians? I’m a Christian.”

“You know, they’ve sort of picked on us through the years. The Inquisition, Nazi Germany, the Soviet Union. To name a few. Let me ask you, when’s the last time you went to church?”

“I can’t remember.”

“That hardly qualifies you as a Christian.”

“What are you, some kind of super Jew or something? When’s the last time you went to a Jewish church?”

“You mean a synagogue?”

“Yeah, that.”

He looked out the window and seemed to stymie a grin. “I can’t remember. Somebody’s wedding, I suppose. Or funeral. I could check my suit pocket when we get back. It might have a program.”

"So why do you care so much about which Jew does what?"

"It's in our DNA. Handed down from generation to generation. Even Jews who don't believe in God? We still care."

It took a second to sink in. "Wait a minute. You don't believe in God?"

He shrugged. "Let's just say I have my doubts."

"Don't you think that's something we should talk about?"

"We're talking about it now."

"I mean, it's kind of important to our future plans, right? Like how we're going to raise our kids."

He shuddered. "Aren't we getting a little ahead of ourselves? Unless there's something you're not telling me."

I shook my head. "Seeing as how we just started doing it, I wouldn't know. Although we've been doing it a lot."

"Is that a complaint?"

"Just an observation."

"Listen, let's continue this discussion over that dinner you're buying me. How about that place?" He indicated a billboard that read "The Golden Calf—Next Exit."

"Looks like a sign from God."

Sure enough, the Golden Calf looked like it had been around since biblical times. So did our server, Milly, who wore her beauty-shop silver-blue hair in a bun and moved like everything hurt. “You kids ready for your ticket?” she asked, eyeballing the retro Coca-Cola wall clock sandwiched between a moose head and a buffalo head. Why restaurant owners thought dead animals would whet our appetites was anybody’s guess.

Aaron shook his head. “Just more coffee, please. We’ve got a long drive ahead of us.”

Milly grimaced and tottered to the coffee maker at glacier speed.

“You want that last onion ring?” Aaron asked.

“It’s all yours.”

He snatched it from the plate and crammed it in his mouth just as Milly returned with the coffee pot and our check.

“So, to recap,” I said after she left, “you’re an agnostic, not an atheist. You’re open to the idea of a higher power, sort of, but you need proof. Isn’t that kind of wishy-washy?”

“I prefer rational.”

“Same difference. But you’re still Jewish, because it’s not just a religion, it’s a race of people with common DNA going back thousands of years.”

“Good. Keep going.”

“And you don’t believe in heaven or hell; you think the most likely scenario when we die is oblivion. One second we’re here, the next we’re on our way to becoming worm food.” The animal heads seemed to peer down in disapproval, perhaps because the rest of them was worm food.

He nodded. “Ashes to ashes, dust to dust.”

“How do you know that? It’s from the Bible.”

"Genesis, to be exact. We wrote it. The Jews, I mean. My parents made me go to Sunday school when I was little."

I brightened. "Mine too!"

"Well, that's one thing we've got," he joked, another reference to "Breakfast at Tiffany's," in my mind rapidly becoming our song.

"I can think of a couple others," I said, ignoring Milly's none-too-subtle scowl from behind the counter. "But seriously, if there's no heaven or hell, what keeps you from doing bad things?"

He drained the last of his water, spitting a lemon seed back into the glass. "Me. It just feels better to try to be a good person. Without some Guy in the Sky telling me I have to."

I had to chew on that for a moment. "But what about Hitler?"

"What about him?"

"If you're right, he's not being punished for all eternity. It's like he got away with everything."

"He's still dead."

"You know what I mean."

Aaron held his hands out imploringly. "I didn't say I had all the answers. That's why I'm agnostic. Maybe der Fuhrer was a tortured soul and his hell was here on Earth. Or not."

"Well, that hardly seems satisfying. Or fair."

"Where in the owner's manual does it say life is fair?"

As if to answer Aaron's question, Milly flipped the Open sign to Closed and said, "He's right, you know. Which is why I'm kicking you kids out of here. Conversation over. Have a nice life."

At that, Aaron slipped one of the dollars he'd left on the table back into his pocket. Fair was fair. And sometimes saved you money.

CHAPTER 10

Day two. We'd been driving almost nonstop, taking turns when one of us started nodding off, pulling into rest areas to catch a few winks.

The road sign just south of Sandy, Utah, read "Las Vegas 398 Miles." If you're just starting out in the morning, that doesn't sound so bad. But when you've been driving practically since sunrise, it warrants a discussion.

"We can still make it if we drive all night," Aaron said.

I chewed on my bottom lip, mulling it over for exactly two seconds. As much as I wanted to see my new home, my aching butt screamed otherwise. "I'm beat. Let's check into a motel and sleep in a real bed. We can start out fresh in the morning."

Aaron didn't even try to protest, so I knew it sounded good to him, too. We followed the highway another few miles until exiting at the first off-ramp promising "Gas. Food. Lodging." There was a joke in there somewhere, but I was too tired to make it. A handful of hand-lettered posters led us into a succession of seemingly random rights and lefts onto narrower and narrower roads (with worse and worse paving) until my little Ford shook like an out-of-balance washing machine. Just before we decided to bail, the path dead-ended at a long gravel driveway winding up a hill to a rustic wooden structure billing itself as the Tranquility Motor Lodge, Juice Bar and Meditation Center. The tires made crunching noises and rocks pinged against the Focus's undercarriage as we pulled up to the main office.

Aaron cast a dubious look my way. "Your call," he said.

"Oh, what the heck. I don't feel like turning around and heading back to the highway this time of night. Who knows? It might be fun."

"That's what Norman Bates' victims said."

"Who?"

Aaron's jaw dropped. "The Bates Motel? *Psycho*? The knife-in-the-shower scene?"

"Sorry. I don't watch those kinds of movies."

"Well, you should. They can save your life." His to-be-continued expression let me know the conversation wasn't over, merely on hold.

As we exited the vehicle, I scooped up the fast-food remnants, potato-chip bags, and cookie wrappers littering the front floor like multicolored leaves and deposited them in a series of recycling bins marked "Paper," "Cans," "Glass and Plastic," and "Trash." Aaron gave the outside area the once-over before deeming it acceptable, or at least not life-threatening, then rang the bell to the right of the front door. It responded with the hypnotic strains of a Native American chant. Moments later, we were greeted by a slim fortyish woman with faraway eyes and waist-length auburn hair held captive by a headband adorned with small turquoise stones. Although older, she reminded me of hippie girls from the Woodstock movie we watched in my college class about the '60s. She sized us up for a few seconds through round spectacles before saying, "Welcome. Do you have a reservation?"

Aaron shook his head and I briefly pictured us spending the night in the car or soldiering on to Las Vegas. "Do we need one?"

Showering us with an angelic smile, she said in a singsong voice, "No, just force of habit, I guess. We have plenty of rooms. Please, come in. I'm Melinda."

Aaron introduced us and we followed her inside to a cramped lobby that looked like a counterculture museum, crammed with Beatles and Hendrix posters, beaded curtains, and more candles than a Buddhist monastery, filling the air with vanilla, rose, jasmine, and a dozen other fragrances I couldn't identify. I wriggled my nose, stifling the urge to sneeze.

After checking us in, Melinda handed us a homemade map of the area and said, "We have more than forty acres with dozens of hiking trails perfect for exploring, picnicking, whatever brings you joy. If you keep your eyes open, you can see anything from squirrels and lizards to larger creatures like coyotes." She must have sensed the look of terror I flashed Aaron, because she added, "They won't hurt you. They're all well-fed and accustomed to humans. All the creatures up here live in balance and harmony with the natural environment. They'll bring you good luck. You might even cross paths with a cow or goat wandering in from the Bradley ranch next door."

"That's more like it," I said. Cows didn't scare me.

She continued, "Tonight, if you sit on the balcony and look up, you'll see a million stars. Not at first, but focus on the first grouping and before you know it, they'll begin popping out as if by magic. Have a little wine, maybe some herb, and I guarantee you'll sleep well. Farther up the hill, jutting out of the ground, is the biggest chunk of magnetite in the region; this whole area is built on magnetic deposits. It's a very healing place. You'll want to check it out tomorrow for sure. I get the feeling you're in a hurry, but it'll be worth it. You'll leave here with your chakras in alignment and a deep feeling of peace in your souls."

I made a mental note to run a Google search on "chakras." I wasn't one hundred percent sure what they were, but "alignment" sounded good to me.

"Oh, and one more thing," she said. "We have a labyrinth for walking meditations at the top of the hill, with the most amazing views of Cedar Valley. You must promise me you'll take advantage of it." She handed me another sheet of paper with the headline, "The Story of the Labyrinth." I folded it up and stuck it in my purse for later.

"That's kind of like a maze, right?" Aaron said. I could tell he thought it was a waste of time.

"That's what people think," Melinda said. "But it's not. A maze is a puzzle. A labyrinth, on the other hand, is a spiritual journey, a metaphor for life. Read the paper I gave you, then walk the pathway. There's no right or wrong way. No matter how you do it, you'll be transformed."

She smiled radiantly as she gave us the key, attached by a coiled lanyard to a piece of wood decorated with the yin-yang symbol. "Enjoy," she said. "And if the spirit moves you, please post a lovely review on Yelp. For some reason, people think we're the Bates Motel."

I awoke at dawn to the crowing of a rooster who was very proud of himself. Maybe he'd had a particularly productive night in the henhouse. Ordinarily, I'd have found him annoying at best, but I felt refreshed and energized. The bed was big and fluffy and inviting, with lots of pillows of every shape and size, many of which found their way onto the floor. In the half-light of early morning, I could see the room looked very much like the front office, featuring a similar eclectic collection of old books and posters and candles. Over the fireplace hung a large rectangular sign with the word "Imagine" crudely carved in the dark wood. Was it some other kind of sign too? After all, I was having a hard time imagining my new life in Las Vegas.

Wriggling out from under the covers, I padded over to the kitchenette and rooted around before finding some kind of coffee/chicory concoction that gave off a woodsy scent and roused Aaron in mid-snore. "What are you burning?" he said, rubbing the sleep from his eyes with two knuckles.

"The house blend. When in Rome, right?"

"Sure. Why not? I wonder if we can find something to eat before we hit the road."

"Um, I was going to ask you about that. I really want to explore this place, try out the labyrinth and the other stuff she talked about. I might not get another chance. What's the latest we can get back?"

He looked disappointed, but said, "Anytime tonight, I guess. But seriously? All that hocus pocus sounded good to you?"

"Yes, actually. I think I was a hippie in a previous lifetime."

He sat up in bed and I handed him an oversized mug. "I could get used to this kind of service," he said with a grin. Blowing on the steaming brew, he took a tentative sip and pronounced it decent. "Too bad we don't have any 'herb.'"

We both laughed and I said, "You noticed that, too. That Melinda's quite a character. But I like her."

"Same here. Okay, I'm sold. We can check everything out before we check out. Hey, that's not a bad idea for a song lyric." He reached for his phone and punched in a few lines. "But first I've gotta get some food in me."

Rifling through the drawers and finding nothing but two small packs of saltines and a broken fortune cookie, we hiked back up to the office, remembering that the name of the lodge included Juice Bar. And sure enough, we heard the whirring of the juicer growing louder as we approached the entrance.

"Good morning," Melinda said. "I'm whipping up a kale, spinach, parsley, lemon, and ginger blend. With just a touch of carrot for sweetness. Interested?"

"Yum," I said. I didn't think I'd ever tried kale before, but my growling tummy insisted. While Aaron looked skeptical, he reached for one too. We finished ours off in greedy gulps and asked for refills, which made Melinda smile more broadly than usual. I made a mental note to buy one of those juicer things you see on the infomercials first chance.

When we'd stopped asking for more, Melinda asked, "Stay for yoga?"

By this time, we'd decided just to go with the flow (a phrase I learned from my mom), so we spent the better part of the morning with several other guests doing postures known as "asanas." I liked cobra best, while Aaron seemed partial to downward-facing dog. Neither of us was particularly adept at standing on one leg (the tree position), although I beat Aaron by three whole seconds. Of course, when I pointed this out, Melinda reminded me that yoga isn't a competition, but a path to personal growth and meditation, which made me look away in shame (not an official yoga pose, BTW).

Later, we explored the grounds, stumbling across lizards, squirrels, and other small creatures scurrying through the brush, but, thankfully, no coyotes. Eventually, we discovered the labyrinth Melinda had told us about, laid out on a clearing atop a hill and made up of smooth black stones forming a spiral of concentric circles. I was eager to try it out and convinced Aaron to let me go first.

"Sure, go for it," he said, probably happy to relax on a weather-beaten wooden bench provided for those waiting their turns.

Racing through the pathways, anxious to reach the center, I found myself frustrated by the many switchbacks impeding my progress. Sadly, it all seemed like a waste of time and energy to me. At the center, I drew a long sigh, stood there for a couple of seconds, and rather than retrace my steps, exited the pattern by leaping over the stones in five giant strides.

"How was it?"

"Disappointing. After Melinda's buildup, I thought I'd discover the secret of life. Or something."

Aaron stood up and stretched. "Maybe I'll have better luck."

In contrast to my own style, Aaron strolled through the formation at a leisurely pace, hands clasped behind his back, often stopping entirely to listen to a sound or simply stare off into the distance. Meanwhile, I found myself growing more and more impatient. "We don't have all day, you know!" I heckled at one point, even though we did. He waved me off, which just increased my agitation. After arriving in the inner circle, he stood there perfectly still, hands on hips, for what seemed like an hour, while I paced back and forth in front of the bench. Finally, he left the center spot, meandering back through the spirals as slowly and deliberately as he'd entered.

"That was amazing," he said finally. I searched his face for any trace of irony, but found none.

"Amazingly boring," I said. Eliciting no hoped-for laughter, I added, "Okay, enlighten me."

"Well, you know how you ran through the circles? For you, it was all about the destination. But once you got there, you couldn't wait to get out. You even took a shortcut. But I moseyed my way through, paid attention to the sights and sounds and smells, really enjoying the journey. I could have stayed there even longer."

"I noticed." I didn't know why, but his explanation was beginning to aggravate me.

He took my hand in his. "No need to get defensive. It's not a criticism."

"I'm not defensive," I started to protest, but thought better of it. There's no way to say that without sounding defensive. Instead, I tried petulant. "Okay, you're obviously much more evolved than I am."

Aaron shook his head. "Melinda said there's no right or wrong here, just different ways of following our paths. It's an awareness thing. Maybe you should slow down and I should speed up. We can meet somewhere in the middle. Get it?" He gazed into my eyes and smiled, and my irritation melted. "I'm glad we decided to stay," he added. "And it's all because of you."

"Ironic, isn't it?" I had to admit. "We've switched roles already."

"Another ah-ha moment. The labyrinth continues to work its magic."

We stood there in silence and gazed across the valley as the sun vanished behind a distant mountain range, leaving a swath of orange and purple in its wake. It would take me awhile, perhaps forever, to get used to these western panoramas. At the moment, they instilled a sense of awe, wonder, and agoraphobia.

"Looks like we're going to be driving at night again, after all," I said.

"Yep, time to go home."

For an instant, I thought he meant Scandia. With a mixture of excitement and regret, I realized he meant Las Vegas. I wondered how long before it felt like home to me.

CHAPTER 11

A gentle prod roused me from my nap.

"Go away," I said, not fully conscious.

Before I could readjust myself in my seat, Aaron said, "Open your eyes. You need to see this."

"What?" I sounded annoyed, even to my own ears.

"Las Vegas. You only get one chance to see it for the first time."

I stretched, repositioned the seat, sat up straight, and stared into the blackness ahead. "You woke me for this?" All I could see in the headlights were carcasses of blown tires, strewn over the highway like rubber roadkill.

"Any minute now. Just over the next hill. In the meantime, look up."

I did as instructed and witnessed what appeared to be a massive oblong object hovering low in the night sky, rays of gold and silver and orange emanating from somewhere deep inside, imbuing it with an otherworldly glow.

I gasped. "Good Lord, is that what I think it is?" It looked like something out of the old *Close*

Encounters movie. Apparently, the desert held more mysteries than I'd ever imagined.

"Depends," Aaron said through a mischievous Cheshire cat grin that made no sense to me. "Keep watching."

As if I could take my eyes off what I was already christening the "Mother Ship." It reminded me of the time we took a family vacation to Niagara Falls. I couldn't have been more than 13 or 14 and a road trip with my parents was the last place I wanted to be—until we turned a corner and I got my first glimpse of a towering wall of water more spectacular than anything I'd experienced to that point in my life.

"Holy cow, that's amazing!" I'd said, not understanding why my mother and father were chuckling. "What's so darned funny anyway?" I added, which only made them laugh harder. "What is wrong with you people?" I guess the "you people" reference pushed them over the edge and now tears streamed down their cheeks competing with the falls, making me feel like my head was about to burst. That was when we banked into another turn that put us directly in front of a waterfall that made the first look like an overflowing bathtub.

"And now you know," my father said, wiping away the last drop of moisture with a hardened hand as he patiently explained the difference between the American and the Canadian falls.

This was a lot like that. I could tell Aaron was messing with me in exactly the same way, although I had no idea why. Gaping slack-jawed right into the UFO, I watched it morph into a cloud, realizing that something of earthly origin accounted for the extraterrestrial iridescence. In some ways, this was actually more incredible than my flying-saucer fantasy. What kind of lights could create that illusion?

And then I knew. As we crested the hill, the source spread before us like a giant bowl of shimmering gemstones, decidedly terrestrial, but no less alive.

“Welcome to fabulous Las Vegas,” Aaron said.

“You sound like the Chamber of Commerce.”

“It’s on our sign.” As he leaned over to kiss me, the car swerved dangerously into the next lane, making boppity-boppity-bop sounds over the speed buttons. A black pickup next to us leaned on its horn and Aaron recovered smoothly, my heart revving faster than our vehicle.

“Sorry.” Aaron offered an olive-branch wave to the driver, but the man had already presented his middle finger. The finger was attached to a muscular heavily tatted arm and I had visions of the arm’s owner following us to wherever we were going and kicking our butts. Which brought up the questions, could Aaron handle himself? And protect me? At a tad under six feet, just this side of too thin, with long ropy arms revealing an impressive network of tendons, I had a feeling he could give as good as he got. Scrappy and probably fast, too. But would it be enough? I filed that away as a topic for another day. We’d discovered so much about each other on this road trip, but a whole iceberg of submerged issues remained. I guessed that was what the next 50 or 60 years were for.

We sat in silence for a few moments while I absorbed the view, coming more into focus with each mile marker. Already, I could pick out individual structures, one that looked like the Space Needle on steroids and another shooting a white beam of light far into the heavens. In response, my leg started twitching uncontrollably and I stifled the urge to pee. Was this fear, excitement, or a heady combination of both?

"What if I hate it?" I asked finally, surprised the question hadn't occurred to me before.

"Las Vegas? Everybody hates it at first."

I couldn't tell if he was kidding. "That's comforting."

"Well, it's true. Despite what our sign says, this isn't the most welcoming place for newcomers. Maybe it's because so many people move here and try to change us. You'll see Nevada bumper stickers that say, 'We don't care how you do it in California.' It's slowed down the past five or six years because of the economy, but it's starting to heat up again. Just keep three things in mind and you'll be fine."

"I'm all ears." I took out my pen and reporter's notebook just in case.

"First, it's Nevada, short 'a' like what's-a-matta. If you say it like regatta, you'll immediately be branded a carpetbagger and shunned for life."

"Seriously? It's that important to people?"

"Sadly, yes. Second, never play slots in the car wash. Or anywhere that's not a casino. They have the lowest payouts in town."

"That won't be a problem." The idea of gambling

held no appeal for me. I had too much respect for money and how hard it was to earn, much less hold on to.

"Good. And finally, stay off Eastern. Or as I like to call it: Effing Eastern. Especially in Henderson."

"Henderson?"

"A bedroom community just south of Las Vegas. Eastern's always a disaster; fender benders, bumper-to-bumper traffic, constant construction, lights never in sync. Just trust me on this one."

I snuggled up to him. "I trust you on every one. That's why I'm here."

He pulled me even closer.

"By the way," I said. "Effing Eastern is a good name for a band."

CHAPTER 12

Aaron lived in a "daily, weekly, monthly," essentially a glorified motel on a road mistakenly named Paradise a couple blocks off the Strip. It might as well have been a thousand miles away. In contrast to the bright lights and endless activity I'd just seen, this place made a minimum-security prison look inviting, with its peeling gray paint, cratered parking lot (with a single brave weed clawing its way out of the asphalt), and gallery of signs prohibiting everything from trespassing and skateboarding to dumping. (I had no idea what that meant and had no intention of finding out.) If I'd been in a better frame of mind, I would have found the No Lifeguard on Duty notice particularly amusing, in light of the absence of water in the pool. For the first time since leaving Michigan, doubts began to creep in like kudzu, wrapping around my brain anaconda-style. Although Aaron had tried to deliver a tepid heads-up somewhere back in Utah, nothing could have prepared me for this extreme culture shock. Still, I made an effort to steel my resolve. I enjoyed camping and sometimes fantasized about living in a tent or RV. At least this place had running water. Right?

"It's not as bad as it looks," he said, sensing my mood while fumbling for his front-door key. His worried eyes searched my face for signs of validation. Finding none, he reached for my hand, perhaps in an effort to prevent me from bolting through the parking lot screaming. As the door swung open, it occurred to me that, no matter the price, this place was nobody's bargain.

Basically one oversized room divided by a half wall with a clunky 1990s-era swivel TV bolted to the top (as if anyone would steal it), the apartment consisted of a tiny bedroom with a full-sized bed taking up most of the square footage, an equally tiny living space, and a kitchenette featuring an easy-bake oven, a bar fridge, and a microwave suitable for popping corn and not much else. Aaron had decorated it like a frat house, with a cinderblock bookcase, a chaise lounge, a stained cardboard box doubling as a trash can, and posters of Linkin Park and Primus on the walls covering only God knew what. Not to mention bass guitars strewn everywhere, leaning like languid mannequins against every inch of available wall space, surrounded by amps and sheet music and cords that might never untangle.

"It's not much, but I call it slum," Aaron said with a feeble smile. That was when I realized he wasn't any happier about his situation than I was. If I truly loved this man, I needed to reassure him now. "It just needs a woman's touch."

He looked genuinely relieved. "We won't be here

long, I promise," he said, cranking up a small window air conditioner that kicked in under protest, spewing a halo of dust into the room.

"We're moving, bro?" a voice boomed from the bathroom, followed immediately by a flush and the creak of a door. And there in the semi-darkness stood the voice's owner, a greasy coil of black hair and nervous energy easily tipping the scale (if he owned one) at 250 pounds, wearing ragged jeans and a tattered yellow T-shirt that read, "Don't Blame Me, I Have Tourettes." He captured Aaron in a bear hug, eliciting an audible umph as he lifted him off the threadbare carpet.

After the big man deposited Aaron back on the ground, Aaron said, "Don't mind Sasquatch, it's just my on-again, off-again roommate, Josh Boozer. ..." Before he could finish, both of them said in unison, "Rhymes with loser." A line they'd no doubt delivered countless times before.

"This is Anna Christiansen, of the Michigan Christiansens," Aaron introduced me. I gave a little curtsy.

"Pleased to meet you." He smiled broadly and presented a hairy mitt. We shook hands and, as soon as he looked away, I wiped mine on my pants. "I've heard so much about you."

His statement surprised me. "Really? When?"

He glanced down at his filthy bare caveman feet like a second-grader caught in a lie. "Uh, actually, I haven't. Isn't that just something people say?"

Aaron came to his rescue, sort of. "Josh is socially challenged. Feel free to hit him. Everyone else does." Turning to his roommate, he said, "And no, we're not moving. I'm moving, Anna and me. You'll have to make other arrangements."

Josh stuck out his lower lip and made it quiver in mock dramatic fashion.

"Don't fall for it," Aaron said to me. "Josh is perfectly capable of fending for himself. Tell her about your new job."

He warmed visibly. "I'm a bathroom attendant at the Heaven's Gate Casino and Wedding Chapel downtown."

My confused expression prompted an explanation.

"You know, I stand there looking all official and give dudes a squirt of soap and a towel after they do their business, and they tip me for my, you know, attentive service. I can pull down fifty to a hundred big ones a shift. Not a bad gig—if you don't mind the smell and the noises."

The image made me cringe. To my knowledge, we had nothing like that back home.

"There's only one problem," Aaron said. "They haven't actually hired him. He just showed up one day and started doing it."

Josh beamed. "True dat. Highly entrepreneurial, don't you think? I must be doing something right, because nobody's run me off yet. I've even gotten tokes from the security guards."

"Tokes?" I asked.

"Tips. Vegas term. I guess they assume I work there. Hey, it's a win/win. The casino looks like a class joint and they don't have to pay me, while I'm making a decent living. What's wrong with this picture?"

"Nothing," I had to admit. In fact, I admired his nerve.

"I like this girl, Aaron," Josh said. "Better than the last one."

Except for the grating of the air conditioner and the sound of my heart cracking, the room fell into an uncomfortable silence.

"Gotcha!" Josh said after a few too many seconds. "You should see the look on both your faces."

I didn't know whether to punch him or kiss him.

Aaron was leaning toward the former. "You're an asshole," he said. "Get the hell out of here and take that stupid lounge chair with you."

Josh shook his head. "Won't be needing it. Today's my Friday. Think I'll head over to Desert View and spend the night curled up in one of those nice comfy waiting-room chairs."

"Desert View?" I took the bait.

"Hospital. If you look worried, they just assume you're waiting for a sick relative." He looked at Aaron, then back at me. "I'm gonna write a book someday."

"He's gonna do a lot of things someday. In the meantime, leave."

"You'll miss me when I'm gone."

"Highly unlikely."

"A pleasure," Josh said as he stepped outside. "I look forward to continuing our conversation. And if you ever find yourself in the men's room of the Heaven's Gate—"

"Out!" Aaron gave him a shove to help him on his way. After locking the door, he said, "Sorry about that. He thinks he's funny. Genetics. His father was a semi-famous comedian here in town. Until they found his body stuffed in a dumpster down in Laughlin, about ninety miles south. I suppose he pissed off the wrong people. If Josh isn't careful, he's going to follow in the old man's footsteps."

"That's terrible. No wonder he's like that."

"I've known him since middle school. He was like that before. Now he's just more like that."

"Well, I think he's charming in a warped I-just-dropped-in-from-another-planet kind of way."

"Wow," Aaron said. "Makes me question your judgment."

"Hey, he's your roommate."

Aaron crossed the room (not exactly a challenging task) and tried to hug me. Instinctively, I pushed him away. "Whoa! Too hot, too hot!"

"What do you mean?" He looked honestly confused.

"I mean, it's the middle of the night and did you see the temperature on that bank sign when we drove in? It said ninety-nine degrees. I've never felt ninety-nine degrees in my life, let alone at this hour."

"Sorry, I forgot this is your first time. You'll get used to it. Your blood will thin."

"How long does that take?"

"Actually, I have no idea. I'm born and raised here. A hundred and ten feels normal to me."

I couldn't grasp the notion, so I just sank into the lounge instead, thankful Josh had declined to take it with him. "While I'm waiting to adapt, can you please get me something cold to drink? I'm parched."

"Sorry. I've been saying that a lot since we got here, huh?" He made the short trip to the kitchen and opened the little fridge. "I have beer and, uh, beer," he said sheepishly.

"Surprise me."

He popped open a couple of tabs before joining me on the chaise. It bucked under our combined weight, but held its ground. "To your new adventure," Aaron said. We clicked cans.

"Our new adventure." The first swig was right out of a TV commercial, transporting me to a cool stream high in the Rockies. To complete the fantasy, I pressed the chilly can against my forehead. "Much better."

"Listen, as long as I'm apologizing for everything, I'm sorry about this place, too. Want to know why I live here? Besides the obvious cost savings?"

"I'm all ears."

"Motivation. I figure the more uncomfortable I am, the quicker I'll need to be successful so I can leave."

I had to admit it made sense—in what I was starting to think of as "Aaron logic."

"We'll get outta here soon," he said, the second time he'd made that promise since our arrival.

"I believe you." And I did. I knew he made more than $40,000 a year and after a quick calculation, I figured that after paying for this dump for a year, he probably had $37,500 left over.

"At least the bed's made. I read a quote from a

Navy Seal that said if you make your bed perfectly every morning, it means you accomplished your first task of the day. You'll have a small sense of pride and you'll be encouraged to complete more tasks. It'll also remind you that it's the little things in life that matter." He paused to take another sip of beer. "And if you happen to have a shitty day, at least you'll come home to a well-made bed. So there's that." He smiled and cupped my chin in his hand. "Wanna test it out?"

"Yes," I said automatically. And to heck with the heat.

CHAPTER 13

"Why do they even bother with the weather?" I greeted Aaron the next day as soon as he came home from band practice. I'd wanted to tag along, but had been informed of their no-girlfriends' policy, also known as the "Yoko Rule," indicating their awareness of music history. He didn't notice the cheap forest-themed art I'd picked up at Target in a failed attempt to make the room homier, and got right to the point.

"Hi. Nice to see you too." He trotted over and planted a friendly kiss on my lips. "What do you mean?"

I pointed to the screen. "The five-day forecast. Every day's the same. Nothing but bright smiling suns."

"Well, it is a desert out there," he said, echoing a TV awareness campaign designed to remind people to save water. It was the reason I turned off the faucet while brushing my teeth, only letting it run when I spit. And it was the same reason Aaron made fun of me, maintaining that my little act of conservation would make exactly no difference, especially because hotels were the big wasters. I didn't care. Apparently, we were in the throes of an endless drought and I was determined to be a good citizen in my adopted city.

"Not many people know this," Aaron continued, "but we do have four seasons."

This was news to me, so I bit. "How so?" I asked, not realizing I was playing straight man to his standup comedian.

"Early summer, summer, late summer."

"That's three," I said, falling deeper into his trap.

The satisfaction on his face was evident. "And next summer."

I gave him a single nyuck. "Don't quit your day job." Then, "I'm serious. I've never been so hot in my life."

He brushed me off. "You'll get used to it."

I felt myself get even hotter. "Hey, I could use a little empathy here. It's hard for newcomers. I'm drinking water constantly. But I hardly ever pee. I'm starting to think I'm diabetic. And the nosebleeds. Maybe it's leukemia. I looked it up on WebMD."

Aaron wrapped me up in his arms and I let him, despite the heat. "Don't pay any attention to those quacks. It's just Vegas."

"If you say so." We smooched for a good long minute.

"Hey, you got a nickel?" he asked randomly.

"Maybe. Why do you ask?"

"How 'bout I take you on the nickel tour?"

~O~

We hopped into Aaron's car, some kind of faded blue Japanese hatchback from the early 2000s that looked like his budget suite on wheels, and drove to Mandalay Bay, a golden-glass monstrosity on one end of the Strip. I had no idea which end, because I hadn't been in town long enough to know my directions. The sun had already gone down, so that was no help, although it gave the illusion of cooling off a degree. Not that it mattered. Before leaving Aaron's, he'd insisted I change into light sweats ("buffet pants," he called them in preparation for the orgy of eating we'd be engaging in later) and comfy sneakers to help with all the walking.

I had briefly wandered through the Greektown Casino Hotel in Detroit right after turning 21. (I always thought it interesting how they listed "Casino" first, a sliver of honesty in a profession built on something else.) But nothing prepared me for Mandalay. It was like going to my first Major League game after watching Double A. You could tuck the entire Greektown building into one corner and hardly notice.

The casino, from the carpet and wall coverings to the lighting, matched the golden hues of the exterior, possibly some sort of subliminal message to gamblers that fortune lurked just around each corner, the push of a button away. I clutched Aaron's hand tightly as we wove our way through a pack of freshly sunburned conventioneers still wearing their "Hi, My Name Is ____" stickers, past drunks slurring rude comments to drunker drunks stabbing at the wrong buttons on ATM machines while others waited behind them for their infusions of cash, and stopping briefly to gawk at a gaggle of Asian tourists whooping it up in front of a long row of a You Might Be a Redneck slot machines. From somewhere in the distance, a cheer rose from a group of mostly male gamblers flanking some kind of table.

"Dice," Aaron said, noticing me stare in that direction, trying to figure out what was going on. "They call it 'craps,' but I call it 'claps'—whenever there's a big noise in the pit, it's coming from a crap table."

"Pit?"

"Oh, yeah, that's the area in the middle of the casino with all the table games."

"Crap. Pit. It all sounds a little too Freudian for me."

No sooner had the noise died down than I heard groans from another table, the vagaries of Lady Luck captured in a single quick sequence. Meanwhile, a crew of young women, one wearing a pink T-shirt emblazoned with the word "Bride" and the others featuring "Bride's Bitches," stumbled around like fawns in heels they hadn't worn since senior prom.

From time to time, the sounds of simulated coins hitting imaginary trays filled the air; Aaron had to explain that the newer generation of slots took greenbacks, but nary a coin. Then he handed me a twenty and pointed me in the direction of an I Dream of Jeannie machine.

"It's my favorite," he said. "Wanna know why?"

"I have a feeling you're going to tell me anyway."

"I like to hear her say, 'Yes, Master.'"

"You're a barrel of laughs tonight." I gave him a playful nudge.

"Go ahead. Take it for a spin. You might hit the jackpot."

"I can't. Where I'm from, twenty dollars is a lot of money. I know how hard it is to make."

"Well, you can't come to Las Vegas without giving it a try. You could be walking around lucky and not know it."

I studied the machine for a moment. "I have no idea where to put this."

Aaron indicated a slot where you inserted the bill. But when I slid it in, the machine spit it right back out.

"Look, that's gotta be some kind of sign," I said, relieved I wouldn't be wasting his money after all.

"It's a sign the paper's too wrinkled." He reached in his wallet and extracted a newer twenty, which the machine was only too happy to swallow with a digital gulp. "Now push the Spin button. Or you can go old school and pull the handle. Either way."

Despite my misgivings, I knew I'd better get it over with. I gave the handle a good hard yank and watched as the colorful reels spun round and round while the Jeannie theme blared like a calliope. After a few seconds, they came to rest with a haphazard assortment of images: a palm tree on an island, a jewel, a magic lamp, the Taj Mahal, and Jeannie herself astride a flying carpet.

"Is that good?" I asked.

Aaron shook his head. "Try again."

I did as I was told with the same result. In less than two minutes, the twenty was history, presumably on its way to line the pockets of Mr. Mandalay himself.

I stood up and backed away from the machine like it was a wasp's nest. "That was, like, no fun at all."

"Good," Aaron said, revealing his true intentions. "Sometimes when people hit it big the first time, they get hooked. They think it's easy. But look at this place. It wasn't built by giving money away. Sure, they'll throw someone a bone from time to time, but only to keep the fantasy going. It's good for marketing."

I regarded the football-field-sized room and realized Aaron was right. Despite sporadic bursts of excitement, most of the players appeared bored, desperate, drunk, or worse. A few younger gamblers seemed like they were trying way too hard to have a good time, downing shots of a crimson substance that reminded me of cough syrup and calling each other "Dude" and "Bro" and "Yo" in testosterone-fueled rasps. It reminded me of the first sorority party I attended in college. Which was also the last sorority party I attended in college.

Earlier, near the ATMs, I'd noticed a sign with the headline, "When the Fun Stops," and an 800 helpline number for problem gamblers. For most of these folks, the fun appeared to have stopped before it began.

"I get the feeling that people like the idea of Las Vegas better than they like the actual place," I said to Aaron.

"And that's what makes you an astute chronicler of the human condition."

"I hate to be a party pooper. But this astute chronicler wants to get out of here. I need some unfiltered air that doesn't smell like coconuts."

We turned back onto the Strip and headed toward a giant pyramid with a beam of white light (hopefully not the same one you see when you die) shooting into space.

"That's Luxor," Aaron said, sounding like a tour guide. "About the same size as its Egyptian counterpart. The beam is the strongest in the world. If you ever get lost at night, just follow the light. And if you get lost during the day, head toward Pyke's Peak." He pointed at the towering phallic erection I had first noticed when we drove into town.

"I don't think I'll need landmarks. I'm sure I can find my way around with the help of Gypsy."

Aaron's eyes narrowed. "Gypsy?"

"It's what I named my GPS."

"You named your GPS?"

"Sure, doesn't everyone?"

"Uh, no. Regardless, you can't count on him. Or her. Or it. Mine has steered me into dead ends, parking lots, and gated communities without an entry code. You can lose a week here just trying to drive around the block. This town is more complicated than it looks. And not as smart as it thinks it is."

I filed that away for future reference, while we

drove past a medieval castle, the Manhattan skyline, a lot of boxy high-rise hotels, and the Eiffel Tower. Then Aaron made a quick left and pulled into a parking garage, stashed the car, and led me back to the street, where he carefully maneuvered me through the crowds (it seemed everyone was heading in the opposite direction). Then we stood next to a big concrete lake in front of a hotel with 10,000 other people waiting for something to happen. Suddenly, I was watching a dazzling lighted fountain display choreographed to opera and Elvis. It was very cool, much more enjoyable (and cheaper) than losing Aaron's twenty. About halfway through the show, I noticed him staring at me instead of the spectacle.

"What?" I asked, feeling unexpectedly self-conscious.

"Nothing."

"Don't give me that. Why are you looking at me that way?"

"It's just cool to see Las Vegas through your eyes. You're not all jaded like me."

"Give it a few weeks," I said, as a borderline homeless street vendor shoved a pamphlet in my hand. Instead of the random Watchtower I received back home, this one featured a lineup of semi-naked women with obvious enhancements and X's strategically placed over their private areas. Not wanting to add to the mounds of X-rated litter covering the sidewalk, I surveyed the immediate vicinity for a trash can, feeling a sudden urge to take a shower. Finding none, I stuffed the flyer in my purse, planning to toss it at the first available opportunity. "That's disgusting," I said, shuddering.

"Just industrious young ladies working their way through med school," Aaron assured me.

"I may be fresh off the turnip truck, but even I don't believe that one." I paused to consider my statement. "I guess I got jaded in record time."

"Know what your problem is?"

"I didn't know I had one."

"You're not urbanized enough. That's why that street guy had no problem invading your space. You need to look like a badass." He reached over with one hand and moved the corners of my mouth into a frown-like position. But as soon as he removed his thumb and forefinger, it popped right back into place. "I want you to practice your resting bitch face in the mirror at least ten minutes a day. You'll get the hang of it."

"I have a better idea. Why don't I just stay off the Strip?"

"Or you can do that." Laughing, he slid my arm through his and we continued to wend our way along the boulevard, past hotels that looked like ancient Rome (if the Romans had scattered buildings around haphazardly with no continuity or planning), Tahiti complete with an ersatz volcano, and something straight out of Robert Louis Stevenson or Gauguin. We ventured inside that last property, as Aaron referred to it, to use the facilities (bigger and nicer than our entire motel room), then bought a couple overpriced drinks. In short order, it occurred to me that, other than the themes and color schemes, the casinos all looked pretty much the same, including the customers. In other words, if you'd seen one, you'd seen them all. I supposed you didn't have much flexibility with slot machines and blackjack tables as the basic design elements.

For me, the real sense of wonder happened outside. Las Vegas, it seemed, was willing to give away a fortune in free entertainment to lure gamblers inside to squander their money. I was only too happy, heading back toward the car, to witness the volcano spew pretend lava in our direction, although the subsequent blast of heat would have been more welcome in winter.

"Hungry yet?" Aaron asked after the volcano went on break.

"Famished. All that walking, you know?"

"Let's hit the Mirage buffet." He led me into the casino, where we soon found ourselves at Cravings, a ginormous purple room with a crazy mixture of aromas representing cuisines from Italy, Mexico, Asia, and a bunch of other countries, all of which made my mouth water like the fountain we'd just seen.

"It's not the greatest," Aaron said, "but it's not bad. And I've got two comps from the last time we played the lounge."

Not bad? You could've fooled me. Back home, we had something called Bjorn's Smorgasbord, featuring greasy fried chicken, overcooked roast beef, and dehydrated potatoes. And peas. Lots of peas. But from the outside looking in, this was an alternate universe. A column of roughly 50 people stood between us and food, but Aaron produced a magic pass that allowed us to walk right up to a cashier at the head of the VIP line. As a pale hostess with a British accent and severe bun led us to our table, I had to admit I felt special, despite (or maybe because of) evil looks from the folks still in line, whom Aaron referred to as "shleppers."

After ordering our beverages, but before heading to the food stations, Aaron offered one piece of advice: "The secret is not to load up on any one thing, no matter how delicious it looks. You'll be tempted, but don't."

"Why?'

"Because you'll crap out before you get to try all the food." He paused for a moment before pointing out a man who appeared to be pregnant with triplets. "Unless you're that guy. Then all bets are off."

"Got it. Can I eat now?"

"Let's go!"

And go we did. Three heaping plates later, I hit the wall, thanking God and Aaron for my sweat pants (which weren't quite so loose anymore).

"I feel sort of guilty about this," I said, watching bus people clear away dirty dishes still piled high with goodies. "All the food. What about the natives starving in Africa my mom used to tell me about? We could send them some dessert."

"Or," Aaron said, "we could eat it ourselves."

Despite my reservations and a vague feeling of disgust, I sampled the brownies, cheesecake, and a piece of baklava so sweet it made my teeth ache.

"That's it, I'm stuffed," I said, pushing away my plate. "Too much of a good thing."

Aaron chuckled. "That should be our new ad

campaign. 'Las Vegas. Too much of a good thing.'"

"Or how about 'Las Vegas. Where puking is just the beginning.'"

He thought it over. "Even better. I'm calling the Convention and Visitors Authority first thing in the morning. We'll be rich."

"I'd settle for comfortable. Let's go walk this off."

By the time we reached the car, I felt a little better. Back on the Strip, we continued north, passing an upscale mall (Aaron was relieved it was closed, although I made a mental note to return at a later date), but we did stop at a shopping center consisting mainly of tacky gift shops selling mugs and keychains and refrigerator magnets, many showcasing endless variations of the iconic Welcome to Fabulous Las Vegas sign. Aaron offered to buy me an Elvis bobblehead as a goof, but I declined, thinking there was a fifty-fifty chance it would fall apart before we got it back to his place. Instead, I purchased a pack of cards, some dice, and a poker chip for my father, a Viva Las Vegas bell and an oven mitt for my mother, plus a Sin City collector's plate for the one remaining space on Auntie's wall.

On the final leg of our trek, I couldn't help but observe that this portion of the Strip had rapidly, in the words of Devo, de-evolutionized, as if we had crossed an imaginary border into some Third World country. And then we were standing at the base of Pyke's Peak. Up close, the hotel and fat concrete legs of the tower looked seedier and more tired than from a distance. And it made me dizzy just looking up. I momentarily contemplated going to the top. But, as if reading my mind, Aaron put a stop to that.

"The top of the tower is over a thousand feet. Spectacular views in every direction. But whatever you do, don't take the express elevator. And especially don't get on the rides."

"Why's that?"

"Because," he said, "they were all built by the lowest bidder."

CHAPTER 14

"So tell me," I said to Aaron the next evening, right after our server doled out custom tableside salads at Hugo's Cellar, a cool gourmet restaurant tucked away in the basement of the Four Queens Casino downtown. I was a little confused, because I thought I was downtown on our tour the night before. But Aaron explained that that was the Strip, which was in the county, and that this part of the city dated all the way back to the early 1900s, when Vegas was founded as a railroad whistle stop. The Four Queens was Aaron's mom's favorite go-to celebration place from the time he was a kid, probably because they gave every female patron a fresh-cut rose, and he insisted on maintaining the family tradition. "Don't keep me in suspense."

"It's good news," he said, leaning forward and taking my hands in his. "The record company thinks we're great and wants to sign us."

"That's fantastic!"

He sort of smiled and I wondered why he wasn't more excited. "Mostly. They can do some things we can't do on our own. Better quality recordings. Increased distribution. More PR. Plus a small advance. But …" His voice trailed off.

"What? You're killing me here."

"They want us to do a hundred and sixty tour dates this year, twice as many as we're doing now. It's all about continuing to build a 'passionate following of likeminded people,' as they call it. I'm not afraid of hard work, but we'd be on the road all the time."

The notion of me being alone in Las Vegas made me feel like a scared little girl, but I tried my darndest to put on a brave face. The last thing I wanted was to stand in the way of Aaron's dream, knowing this could be his final chance. "Maybe I could go with you. Might be fun, a new adventure."

"You'd hate it. Not at first, but soon enough."

I put down the breadstick I'd just buttered. "How can you be so sure?"

"Because I hate it. You've seen our bus. It's no kind of life for a sane person, driving all night, eating crap food, living out of a suitcase, catching some Z's in motels that make the one back in Scandia look like the Ritz. Plus, you've caught Rob's act. These guys are like my brothers, but there's a lot of sibling rivalry. And before you know it, you and I'll be at each other's throats. Guaranteed."

"Guaranteed? Really?"

"I've seen it happen. Rob's ex-wife. And AJ's ex-fiancée."

I refused to give in to the tears pooling up in

the back of my eyes. "Well, I could fly in to meet you on your days off. And if you get a break in your schedule, you can come home. We can make this work, I know it."

Aaron still looked skeptical, but said, "I believe you. Love is all you need, right?" He paused to take a bite of his made-to-order salad, which, for some unfathomable reason, contained anchovies.

"Right," I said. "I think I heard that somewhere."

Aaron, being the good guy he is, said, "So how was your day?"

"Pretty spectacular. The local PBS station retained me as a freelancer to help with research and fact-checking on their monthly magazine. Not a lot of money to start, but it's a great opportunity. I plan to impress them fast."

"You will, too. And it took you only a day to land a job, not an easy proposition in this city. I'm really proud of you."

"As well you should be. A couple more freelance gigs like that and I can cobble together a decent living, really help us out."

Instead of saying more, Aaron let go of my hands, pulled the plastic stirrer from his margarita, and made a loop by inserting one end of the straw into the other.

"I had a thought," he said, slipping the loose band onto my ring finger. "Will you marry me?"

CHAPTER 15

Even as a young girl, I was never the kind to fantasize and plan out my storybook Prince Charming wedding. Still, my palms hadn't stopped sweating since Aaron's impromptu proposal. And I surely didn't take into consideration that we'd known each other less than a week, or ask myself how I would tell my parents. I knew my mom would be heartbroken and my dad would be beyond pissed, but that was one of a mounting number of bridges I'd cross when I came to them. In my current state of mind, it was all part of the rock 'n' roll whirlwind that had become my life.

Also, apparently, Las Vegas is the easiest place on Earth to get married, short of some Third World village where saying, "I marry you, I marry you, I marry you," allegedly does the trick. The marriage-license office does a booming business right up to midnight (still a couple hours away).

After walking the relatively short distance from the Four Queens, Aaron and I fell into line behind a flannel-and-denim-clad cowboy and his beauty-queen fiancée who, as it turned out, had just met earlier that evening at something called the Sin City Beer Fest (still wearing their green all-you-can-drink wristbands). The thing I was learning about my adopted town: There's always someone to make you feel better about yourself.

Ahead of them stood every possible combination of couple: old and young, gay and straight, white and ethnic, foreign and domestic. America's diversity in the flesh, something I'd never seen in Scandia where most of us looked like Vikings. For some reason, it gave me hope for the future, even though most of these marriages looked like they had the shelf life of a carton of milk.

"About a forty-five-minute wait to get your license," the cowboy slur-drawled in our direction, giving his bride-to-be a pat on the butt. "Then you basically walk across the street to the Marriage Commission and wait in another line. You folks have a witness? You're gonna need one."

Aaron said, "Thanks, bud," pulled out his cell phone, and hit speed dial. "Boozer, it's me. Get your ass over to ..." He held up his phone and yelled, "Anyone know the address here?"

A half-dozen people shouted the answer. "Three-thirty South Third Street, sixth floor!"

Aaron continued. "Hear that? Good. I need a witness. No, I'm not in trouble. No, neither are you. Not yet anyway. Just be here in an hour. Dude, I'm getting married!"

Except perhaps for the cowboy and beauty queen, it was the world's shortest engagement. At least we finished dinner; they told us they'd barely downed four beers.

The ceremony, if you could call it that, consisted of the most generic of vows, the kind you'd see on a TV reality show (which we were quickly coming to resemble), delivered by a bald pale officiant (the Assistant Associate Commissioner of Civil Marriages), a man who looked like all his features had been squeezed into the lower third of his face.

Boozer stood there in his usual shorts and flip-flops, wearing a black T-shirt with the words "Off My Meds" screened across the front. No doubt his idea of formal attire.

The whole thing was easy-peasy, although not for the cowboy and his bunny, who were too inebriated to make the cut. Yes, even Las Vegas has standards, surprising as it probably sounds. We, on the other hand, were in and out in 10 minutes (two of which involved the kiss) and back on the street as Mr. and Mrs. Aaron Eisenberg, a moniker that would take some getting used to, but in a good way.

Boozer had wrangled free drink tickets for the Fireside Lounge in the Peppermill, an iconic location just a quick drive down the street on Las Vegas Boulevard.

"Don't thank me," he said. "Consider it my wedding gift to you crazy kids."

"Not thanking you won't be a problem," Aaron said.

Walking into the building gave me an instant feeling of déjà vu. "I feel like I've been here before."

While Boozer whistled the "Twilight Zone" theme, Aaron explained, "You have, sort of. They shot scenes from the movie *Casino* right here in the lounge. Plus a bunch of other films I can't remember."

"*Showgirls*," Boozer said. "Although I mainly watch it two minutes at a time."

Aaron held out his hands in a pleading manner. "Don't even listen to him."

We planted ourselves around the Fireside Lounge's signature attraction: a fire pit with gas flames dancing out of a pool of electric-blue water. The effect was hypnotic, made more so by our 64-ounce Scorpions consisting of, according to our server, gin, a couple different rums, some fruit juices to disguise the flavor, and a pineapple ring for make-believe nutritional value, all presented in a glass the size and shape of a fishbowl. It only took a few sips before I couldn't feel my lips. Two more and I couldn't feel my brain. Good thing Aaron and I were sharing.

Boozer, meanwhile, drained his in three gargantuan gulps, then snatched an abandoned half-empty Miller Lite from a neighboring table as a chaser. And then, for good measure, took a chomp on someone else's garnish pickle.

"Dude, that's disgusting. Even for you," Aaron said.

"It's good to take the old immune system out for a spin every now and then," Boozer said, reaching into his black duct-tape wallet and pulling out one sad faded dollar bill. "Here, let me help with the tip."

Aaron waved him away. "Apply it to your half of the rent. Which you don't pay."

Amazingly, Boozer found another half-empty brew, this time a Corona, and held it aloft as he said, "A toast. To Aaron and Anna. There was a young lady from Montana— "

Aaron hit him in the eye with a pretzel, derailing his limerick.

Boozer picked it up off the table and stuffed it in his mouth, disposing of it in one chomp. "Okay, let's try again. To the happy couple. It just goes to show, sometimes you do buy the cow."

I hit him in the other eye.

~O~

We drove to the Monte Carlo, where the VIP host owed Aaron a favor for getting him floor tickets to Imagine Dragons, one of Las Vegas' most successful home-grown bands. Before we knew it, we were riding the elevator up to the honeymoon suite on the 28th floor.

As Aaron scooped me up for the traditional crossing of the threshold (the only thing traditional about the night's festivities), Boozer engulfed both of us in his yeti arms, scooped us up, and ferried us into our room, delivering us, laughing, onto the carpet with a thud. The suite was larger, and a lot nicer, than Aaron's budget studio, with an oversized bed, Jacuzzi tub spacious enough for Jonah and the whale, and a picture window overlooking the bright lights of the Strip.

Boozer fell into the couch with a grunt, seriously taxing its structural integrity, and said, "You guys can have the bed. I'm fine right here."

Aaron answered him in one word: "Out!"

Boozer looked pained. "Dude, I haven't even ordered room service yet."

"Out!" I echoed.

He tramped toward the door like a man wearing concrete boots. Turning to face Aaron a final time, he said, "Did you bring protection?"

"Out!" we yelled in unison as the door clacked shut.

PART TWO

July—October

CHAPTER 16

I used to like the smell of gasoline. Call me weird, but it reminded me of road trips we took when I was little and sometimes of my father when he came home from working at the construction site. But this morning, as I pumped gas at the Swiftee Mart on east DI (Desert Inn, for you non-locals), the fumes triggered my gag reflex and I found myself fighting back the urge to puke. Luckily it passed quickly and I was ready to jump back in my car and head over to the research library at UNLV when a digital error message on the heavily scratched screen informed me I needed to see the cashier for my receipt.

Ordinarily, I wouldn't care about the receipt. But since Aaron and I were pinching pennies, taking every tax advantage seemed like the prudent thing to do. Hence the little piece of paper I would eventually throw in a shoebox on our dresser.

As I entered the store, a middle-aged man with a face like a mugshot looked up from the newspaper he was studying behind the cash register and gave me the evil eye, as if I were interrupting some important financial decision. Just then, the greasy stench of cheap hot dogs and cheaper imitation cheese product assaulted my nostrils like a commando brigade, ratcheting up the whole gag thing.

Looking for a restroom sign and finding none, I managed to spit out a desperate question to the counter man, just as a sickening flow of acrid bile made its presence felt in the back of my mouth.

"Sorry," he said in an indeterminate accent as he slowly shook his head. "We do not have facilities in this establishment."

A dozen questions pinged my brain, the most urgent being, "Well, where do *you* go?" In the plastic potted plant in the corner, perhaps?

"Where I do my business is none of your business," he said, returning to his paper.

Before I could verbalize a follow-up inquiry, I did something else instead.

I projectile-vomited all over the counter. And all over him. And then I left. Only later did I realize he still owed me a receipt.

CHAPTER 17

Three "yes's" can't be wrong. One for each time I peed on the First Reaction pregnancy stick. Scientific proof that my newly acquired tummy trouble wasn't all in my head. I sat on the toilet and held up all three at once, a jumble of confused feelings triggering their own version of morning sickness. A baby? We weren't trying. But we weren't being overly cautious either. More like letting nature take its course. Which she certainly had been all too happy to do.

I've heard it said that if you wait until the perfect time to have a baby, you'll never have one. So there was that. And despite all my misgivings, not the least of which was knowing the father, my husband, for less than two months, there was no denying the warm gooey feeling originating in my chest and radiating through my body like sunshine.

I'd tell Aaron as soon as he got home. And my parents, of course. And Auntie. Or would I? They were probably still getting used to the notion of me being gone. I'd put them through a lot already.

Heck, they didn't even know we'd gotten married. My brain said, "Call," but my gut told me it was better to wait. And since my gut would be calling the signals, I decided to listen to it.

For the time being.

CHAPTER 18

"I have news," I told Aaron as soon as he picked me out of the crowd at the Terminal 1 baggage carousel. He looked tired, but healthy, after his first four weeks on the road. We hugged and kissed long enough to miss his bag twice, ignoring the various "get-a-room"-style comments from onlookers who were obviously jealous.

When we took our first break, Aaron said, "Me, too. News, I mean."

"You go first."

"No, you."

"I insist."

"Okay, here goes," he said. "I've had plenty of time to think. We need to buy a house, start living like real people. My crappy little place has served its purpose long enough. And now's a good time, since inventory's high and interest rates are still low." He studied my features like an archaeologist examining an old Roman coin. "So, what do you think?"

I thought it was pretty freaking amazing. "Perfect timing. I'm pregnant."

"Great. I know you're sick of the apartment and—" He did an actual double take, the only one I'd seen outside the movies. "What?"

"Pregnant. Baby. You know, family. You must have heard about it in school. Or NPR."

"Wow," he said. And then said it again, in case I missed it.

I couldn't tell if it was a good or bad wow. He looked like he'd been smacked in the head with a blunt object. But then he held me for like a week, not saying a word, and I had my answer.

"Well, that settles it," he said finally.

"Settles what?" I asked, although I had a pretty good idea already. I braced myself for the reply.

"The tour. I can't possibly go back on the road now. Not with all this going on."

I swallowed hard, guilt already tugging at my sleeve. "Sure you can. People do it all the time." Weak. Public defenders made more compelling arguments for clients caught in the act. On video.

"I guess I'm not people."

I rallied. "And that's one of the things I love about you."

He blew right past it, today clearly not a day for flattery. "Look, it's my career. And it's not really going anywhere except endless Bumfuck, Egypts. If anything, I'm relieved. My place is here with you." He patted my tummy. "And our boy."

"Boy? And what makes you think she's a boy?"

"I don't think. I know."

"You don't say!"

"I do. How much you want to bet?"

"No fair. You know I think gambling's a waste of money. And time."

"Sure, Anna, but we'd just be paying ourselves. It's not like we'd lose it to the casino or anything. Call it a hundy?"

"What's a hundy?"

"Hundred bucks. A Benjamin."

"I'll think about it."

Bag in hand, he started off toward the exit, leaving me to ponder the gender, the wager, and a bunch of practical questions for another time as I followed in his wake. Only one thing was certain. We were smart people. We'd figure it out.

❧O☙

No sooner had we entered our place, looking even shabbier now that we were short-timers, than Aaron shouted, "Boozer! Pack your bags! We're moving!"

From the bathroom, where he spent an inordinate amount of time not bathing, Boozer boomed, "Bro, that's awesome! Where we going?"

"Not 'we,' us. As in Anna and me. Time you learned to fly on your own, little bird."

Boozer flushed the toilet in response, signaling an end to the discussion for now.

It hadn't occurred to me we'd be jettisoning our soon-to-be former roommate during the home-buying process. Today was turning out to be not so bewildering after all.

CHAPTER 19

"I want this house."

Our Realtor shuddered. But I stood my ground.

We'd been looking at properties all day and I could feel myself growing more frustrated by the second. Basically, I wanted to scream. But the people in the car didn't deserve that.

The problem was, nothing we'd seen reminded me even remotely of the homes in Scandia. In fact, this part of Nevada couldn't have been more different than Michigan if it were on the moon. When I first moved here, I thought that was a good thing. Now I wasn't so sure.

To begin with, every house looked essentially the same. Outside, some variation of an earth tone, a red-tile roof, and a mottled textured coating they call "stucco." All accented with a patch of "desert landscaping," meaning rocks, cactus, and other bushes that require less than a thimble of water to survive. One house had an impossibly green lawn that, on closer inspection, turned out to be artificial, what Aaron called "AstroTurf." Just thinking about it made me sad.

Inside, more neutral colors, from the carpeting and tile to the walls. Some even had fireplaces! Hotter than hell nine months of the year and local homebuilders thought that wood-burning hearths would be a nice touch to go with the 24-hour-a-day air-conditioning.

Earlier that day, I'd experienced a fleeting twinge of hope (and, yes, homesickness) as we passed a charming red-brick structure surrounded by mature landscaping.

"That's what I'm looking for!" I said, pointing like a child.

Aaron shook his head and chuckled. "You're so cute," he said. "That's a Mormon church."

Libby Silver, our real estate agent, kept riffling through her stack of computer printouts and saying things like, "This one looks promising. An attractive three bedroom, two-and-a-half bath remodel in the Green Valley Ranch community, close to shopping, schools, churches—"

I cut her off. "I think I've seen enough for one day."

Libby had baited and switched us, sort of. On her website and billboards, she appeared to be a young attractive go-getter. In real life, she could be that Libby's grandma. And she moved accordingly, which did nothing to quell my impatience. Either she was Photoshopped up the wazoo or that picture was taken during the '90s. The 1890s.

"I understand," Libby said at last. "I'm sure I've managed to confuse the heck out of you kids. Usually, I don't like to show more than four houses in one day. But it's so beautiful out and you seem like such a nice young couple, I got carried away. We can pick up again tomorrow morning if you'd like."

As she attempted to take us back to Aaron's apartment, Libby succeeded in getting us mired in an endless maze of detours. Las Vegas, I'd learned, is famous for these. You can leave the house in the morning and your street is just fine. By the time you return in the evening, a fleet of gigantic earthmovers has chopped it into a million pieces and a battalion of city workers with shovels and orange flags have taken up semi-permanent residence in the one-remaining lane.

Libby had just made an ill-advised turn into an older neighborhood (which in Las Vegas means the 1950s), when we came to a sudden stop behind a flatbed truck loaded down with massive concrete pipes. The late-afternoon sun beat mercilessly through the windshield, somehow managing to miss the four-inch strip of tint lining the top, making the a/c more ineffective than ever. Why someone would drive a Volvo in the desert is beyond me. What could the Swedes possibly know about temperatures in excess of a hundred and ridiculous?

"I'm so sorry," Libby said. "I have got to get a new GPS."

I briefly entertained the idea of flinging the door open and bolting from the back seat. But the car had childproof locks (which also work on adults). That was when I glanced to my right and saw the house.

It was big, at least two stories. Built of brick.

Tan brick, but brick nonetheless. It looked solid, like a fortress, with a massive green-shingled roof and a wrought-iron fence wrapped completely around the perimeter. While it was nothing like the houses in my hometown, it appeared equally out of place in Las Vegas. For some reason, it made me feel safe. And it had a "For Sale" sign in the front yard.

"Let's check that one out," I said. For the life of me, I couldn't figure out why my heart pounded so insistently.

Libby consulted her paperwork again, rubbed her eyes, and frowned. "Three-thirty-nine East St. Louis. I don't have a sheet on this. It's probably not in your price range. And to be honest with you, this isn't the greatest neighborhood, basically in the shadow of Pyke's Peak."

Aaron agreed. "I grew up around here. This street has definitely seen better days."

"I don't care," I said, about three seconds away from a tantrum.

They must have sensed my hormonal mood (but were wise enough not to say anything), because Libby made a sharp turn into the driveway.

"Besides," I continued, trying to sound reasonable, "it beats staying stuck in this traffic."

Libby released us from the back seat and I semi-jogged to the front gate. Locked. In frustration, I gave it a good shake. It held fast. The metal was hot enough to scorch my palms and leave two black smudge marks for good measure. While Libby went to search for the lockbox, Aaron wrapped his arm protectively around my waist and pulled me closer.

"Looks interesting," he said, smiling. His touch had a calming effect.

I returned his smile. "I can't wait to see the inside. I have a feeling it's amazing."

As if on cue, Libby returned triumphantly with the key. "Let's find out," she said.

It took four tries to insert the key in the lock, and three more to get it to turn. I stood there with arms folded, tapping my foot, trying hard not to shriek. I've always been an easygoing person, so I wasn't exactly enamored of the pregnant me.

In slow motion, the lock gave way with a grumble. Not a moment too soon. For some reason Libby looked alarmed, but pushed the gate open anyway. It squealed in protest, but I didn't care. It was all I could do not to knock her over on my way to the door. But even I knew that would do no good. After all, she had that key, too.

We waded through what looked like a year's supply of yellowing newspapers, dead leaves, torn pizza flyers, and cobwebs to reach the front door, which was actually the side door. It was tall, twelve feet or higher, to match the house. What didn't match was the coat of red paint, now faded to a sickening pink and peeling after too many years in the sun. I wondered if I might look like that after a few more Las Vegas summers.

Again, Libby struggled with the key. What kind of Realtor didn't know how to open a door? An ancient myopic one, perhaps. Maybe I could get

Aaron to kick it in, like on "Cops." But that was just the pregnancy talking. My rational self realized that probably wouldn't make too good of an impression on the sellers.

Finally, finally, finally. The door swung open to reveal the opposite of "amazing." In its place? An endless interior in the final throes of decomposition, from the decrepit kitchen island tilting at a precarious angle to water-stained ceilings, peeling paint, and buckling floors.

The air hung heavy, the fetid aroma of swamp hammering us like a backhand to the face, emanating from a swimming pool that started in the back yard, continued under a glass partition, and ended in the king-size master bedroom, a foot of black water providing a breeding ground for malaria, if that was even possible in the desert. Skittering noises followed by an unsettling wail prompted the three of us to jump back a step as the largest ugliest rat I'd ever encountered (it made Scandia rodents look downright adorable by comparison) chased an overmatched alley cat across the kitchen floor and out through a broken window.

"I've seen enough," Libby said in a voice that sounded close to tears. "I'll wait out here."

Aaron and I were about to join her when a scene flashed before my eyes, showing me the house as it had appeared in its heyday and might possibly appear again. In a fraction of a fraction of a moment, it all unfolded before me, as new as a fresh coat of paint and as cool as the house in *Home Alone*. From what I guessed to be 1960s' appliances, including a soda-fountain counter with hidden blender that popped up from the countertop at the push of a button and a walk-in shower that converted to a steam room with the turn of a knob, it was as though I'd been transported back in time in that crazy *Back to the Future* DeLorean. And anchoring it all in one of two great rooms, a floor-to-ceiling rock fireplace, larger than my dorm and better suited to a Tudor castle.

"Can you picture it?" I asked Aaron, wondering if maybe he'd experienced the same vision.

"All I can picture is the work," he said, and my heart sank. "And the money. But I have to admit, it's a pretty cool place. And luckily, I might be the only Jew on the planet who's good with tools. I think we can do a lot of the rehab ourselves."

We spent the next half-hour dashing from room to room (the upstairs more like a self-contained apartment with its own separate entrance and five or six bedrooms), taking notes and photos, with Libby Silver occasionally calling out, "Hello? Yoo-hoo? Are you ready to leave yet?"

Finally, we met her outside, pacing back and forth in an obvious state of distress. That was when I told her I wanted the house. I could tell she was conflicted. On the one hand, she had the opportunity to make a sale. On the other hand, she'd probably earn every penny of it ... and more.

Neither Aaron nor I knew much about real estate. But we were about to learn fast.

❧ CHAPTER 20 ❧

I won't bore you with all the gory details (mainly because I don't understand them myself), except to say the deal took forever and almost fell through a dozen times. There's a life lesson in there somewhere: The more you want something, the harder it is to get. From what I gathered, it had something to do with defaults and short sales and senior liens and junior loans and other jargon that, no matter how much research I attempted, all looked like gobbledygook to me.

And because we were going for an FHA mortgage, it came attached with all kinds of catch-22 conditions. For example, the house, all 6,700 hundred square feet of it, could never pass an inspection, because the indoor/outdoor pool desperately needed re-plastering, among other things. But the rules prohibited us from doing it, because we weren't yet the rightful owners. Same with all six toilets in all six bathrooms, none of which worked, and the floors that were mostly bare concrete. All this and more turned a simple transaction into a drawn-out ordeal.

Fortunately, Libby Silver, whom I had seriously misjudged, took pity on us and let us in to do the work, putting her license and career in jeopardy. I had no idea why she did that, other than she was really nice. And I cried a lot. Maybe we reminded her of her own kids, or grandkids—or even herself when she was our age. In any event, she looked the other way while we snuck in and, thanks to a copy of *Home Maintenance for Dummies* and some carefully selected YouTube videos, managed to complete most of the needed repairs. I'm sure I cut quite a figure at the bottom of the pool, with my burgeoning belly and breasts (not the worst thing), looking like a manatee with a trowel, at least in my own mind. This was one prenatal activity I wouldn't be sharing with my OB/GYN.

And there was still the matter of money. Even with Aaron pulling down a regular paycheck since officially walking away from the Dickweeds and getting a steady gig with the lounge band Meltdown, we had to come up with a down payment north of $12,000, which might as well have been a million, at least to me. But when I mentioned it to Aaron—more than once, I might add—he sidestepped the question with a wimpy, "It'll be okay," or "Don't worry about it," or "We'll figure something out." When I finally couldn't stand it anymore, he hemmed and hawed and looked at the ground before mumbling into his sleeve, "I have a confession to make."

I folded my arms and tried to look stern. "And what might that be?"

“I, uh, have a small trust fund. My mother left it to me. For situations just like this, apparently.”

“How small?”

“Thirty thousand. Enough to cover the down payment. And the repairs.”

I didn’t know whether to kiss him or kick him. I opted for the kiss, but added, “Why am I just now hearing about this?”

“Well,” he said, “I didn’t want you marrying me for my money.”

CHAPTER 21

I've never thought of myself as materialistic. But when Libby Silver handed over the keys to our new home, elation spread through me like a brush fire. She also brought us a fruit basket and a bottle of non-alcoholic champagne, which she couldn't lay on our counter (next on our to-do list) for fear of it toppling to the floor.

"To you and your new life," she said, toasting us with a plastic glass.

We lifted ours and clinked as best we could. "We couldn't have done it without you, Libby," Aaron said.

She gave us a self-satisfied smile. "Damn straight."

The phony champagne was better than expected, but what I really needed was a chocolate shake from Luv-It Frozen Custard on Oakey just around the block. So I sent Aaron on that important mission, while Libby and I engaged in small talk. He stumbled back in an hour later wearing a sheepish expression and a stain on his pants.

"What took you so long?" I asked. The thought of that shake had made the hour seem like a week.

"Long line."

"Really? At this time on a Sunday?"

"Well, I actually made it home the first time a half-hour ago. But when I pulled into the driveway, the shake tipped over and spilled. So I went back for another."

"Smart boy," Libby Silver said.

"Here, I got one for you, too," he said, handing her a cup brimming with the precious substance.

"You're my hero," I said, tucking into my cup with the biggest spoon I could find.

He favored me with a theatrical bow. "I am but your humble servant." And headed for the door.

"Where are you going, peon?" I asked in a terrible English accent.

"To clean my front seat."

CHAPTER 22

We were six days into the next phase of our home-refurbishing campaign with no end in sight. Already, we'd ripped out what was left of the carpets and broken up all the institutional-white bathroom tile, which reminded me an awful lot of high school, right down to the cracks and stains. We peeled away the red- and gold-foil wallpaper, carried a ton of garbage to the curb (I made a mental note to give the trash guys a little something extra in their Christmas stockings), and caulked a lot of holes in the walls, which led to some entertaining seventh-grade-level wordplay. If this were a movie, you'd see it as a 40-second montage showing just the fun parts, rolling to the soundtrack of Bright Eye's "First Day of My Life," when in actuality it was darned hard work, especially for someone in my "condition." Fortunately, Aaron, who turned out to be even better with his hands than I thought, did the heavy lifting, while I was relegated to doctor-approved tasks like sweeping and supervising.

Here's a scene that would make the final cut.

Toward a midafternoon while waiting for our second wind, Aaron decided he was too tired to drag his butt over to the outlet to unplug the industrial-strength rental vac he'd just used to subdue the walk-in closet (more like a small condo) in what would be our master bedroom. Instead, propped up in the corner, sipping from a can of Coke trickling with condensation, he gave the cord a good yank, not only freeing it from its previous confinement, but causing it to fly across the room like a guided missile before coming to rest squarely on his nose with a sickening thump. The look of shock and pain on his face, not to mention all the blood, should have prompted me to race across the room to his side, offering equal parts Kleenex and sympathy.

Instead, I laughed. And not just any laugh, but a deep seal-like explosion interspersed with desperate gasps followed by hot convulsive tears. Aaron's previous expression was nothing compared to the tidal wave of hurt and anger overpowering his features, as he came to the realization that my wholly inappropriate response was, in fact, not that of a loving wife, but of a crazy person. Which made me laugh even harder.

Later, I chalked it up to pregnancy-induced hysteria when, in reality, it was the fault of the Three Stooges. I know, girls aren't supposed to like Larry, Moe, and Curly. But some of my earliest memories involve getting up early on Saturday mornings and sneaking downstairs to watch TV, and not "Scooby Doo," but a trio of black-and-white knuckleheads who kept poking one another in the eyes and bonking the others on the noggins. I had to cackle into the couch pillow to keep from waking my parents. And now, gazing on my husband covered in a stratum of sweat-streaked white dust and bleeding from the nose, looking for all the world like the Pillsbury Doughboy after a particularly nasty baking accident, I knew it was over. Aaron would have no choice but to dump me on the spot and make me fend for myself on the long, sad, lonely drive back to Michigan.

But then, something magical happened. Aaron started to laugh right along with me, a little snicker at first, which soon turned into a roar that matched mine in decibels and duration. And that was when I knew, really knew, I had the best guy on the planet.

That was also when Boozer walked in carrying a used toilet.

"You shouldn't have," I told him after the tomfoolery (one of my father's favorite words) died down for good. The laughs had gone on at least another two minutes, erupting at irregular intervals like hot spots from a forest fire, threatening to blow up in our faces at the first hint of a breeze. It left me with an ache in my side that was exceeded only by the pain in my jaw.

Here's something you need to know about Boozer. He's got a huge heart. You can't see it inside all the rough edges; in fact, he's essentially one big rough edge. But he'd do anything for you. If Aaron and I ran out of gas in the middle of the desert at 3 a.m., Boozer would drop everything and show up with a pizza and six pack. Of course, he'd forget to bring gas, but at least we wouldn't be hungry or thirsty anymore. So the toilet had to be his idea of a noble deed.

"It was nothing," he said, beaming with pride.

"No, you shouldn't have, seriously. We've got the bathrooms covered."

The immediate downgrade in his expression made me regret my thoughtless remark. Seemingly, I was becoming all too adept at hurting people's feelings.

"I'm sorry," I said, gesturing toward Aaron. "We've had kind of a rough day."

Aaron attempted a smile and fell way short. "You can say that again."

Boozer brightened. His moods changed faster than any human I'd encountered over the age of two. Whipping out his cell phone, he pointed it at Aaron and snapped a succession of quick shots, the virtual shutter approximating the auto advance of a real camera.

"Dude, if that winds up on Instagram, I'm going to have to kill you," Aaron said, trying to struggle to his feet before sitting back down with a soft plop.

"Yeah, I can see how that could happen. If you could actually get up, I mean."

I circled back to the original topic of conversation. "Thanks for the potty."

"It's vintage, circa 1985. You have no idea how hard these things are to come by. I had to pull in some serious favors to get my hands on this baby. Luckily, I know a guy who knows a guy."

"You always do," I said. "So what's the big deal?"

Boozer set the toilet down gently and sat on it as he explained the big deal in the style of a deranged college professor holding court before a packed auditorium of bewildered freshmen. Aaron, who no doubt had witnessed this type of thing before, rolled his eyes, possibly the only movement he was still capable of performing.

"Back in the early nineties, low-flow toilets starting gaining in popularity among your environmentally correct crowd. Whereas the traditional thrones used as much as three-and-a-half gallons of water per flush, the new ones were standardized at one-point-six. Great in theory, not so much in actual practice. Because you had to flush the newfangled ones a minimum of three times to achieve the same results. Do the math. Three flushes times one-point-six gallons equals four-point-eight gallons, a net loss of nearly one and a half-gallons per, uh, load. Once again, the actions of a handful of do-gooders, however well-intentioned, created a chain reaction of unintended consequences that had the opposite effect from its original purpose. Meanwhile, legislation in state after state, beginning with the People's Republic of Massachusetts, mandated the usage of low-flow models, first for new construction and then for existing structures. Government intrusion at its most heinous."

"Know what you need?" Aaron said. "A Power Point."

"Hush. You'll thank me next time you drop a vile deuce. Not a bad name for a band, by the way." Boozer pretended to scan the nonexistent crowd. "Any questions? Answers? Signs of life?"

I held up my hand.

"Yes? The pregnant woman in the back."

"That's a dangerous assumption," I said. "How do you know I'm not just fat?"

"Well, I have access to inside information." He glanced at Aaron who shrugged and grimaced. "What is your question?"

"Is this going to be on the final?"

Boozer peered up from his dollar-store glasses like a scholarly Fred Flintstone and said, "Young lady, everything is going to be on the final."

CHAPTER 23

As promised, I played the dutiful daughter and called my parents every week. With minor variations, the conversation went essentially like this.

"Hi Mom."

"Anna! How are you? It's so good to hear your voice."

"I just talked to you last Saturday. And the Saturday before that."

"I know, dear. Seems longer. We miss you. You'll understand when you have a child of your own."

Well, there was an opening if I ever heard one. But I wussed out and kicked the can down the road. "I miss you, too."

"Let me get your father. He's in the basement working on one of his model boats. Frankly, the noise is driving me crazy."

"Don't bother him."

"No bother at all. He'll be upset if he finds out he missed your call. Hang on."

When she put the phone down, I could hear the sound of his jigsaw escaping from the subterranean workshop. Then footsteps and throat-clearing.

"Hi, honey. It's your father."

"I know, Dad."

"How are you?"

"Good. How are you?"

"Good. Uh, are you keeping your nose clean?"

In my dad's world, few things were more important. "Yes, Dad. I'm walking the straight and narrow." Speaking his language.

Awkward pause. Then, "Good. So is that young man of yours treating you well?"

"Yes. He's a lot like you."

I could almost picture the tiniest of smiles attempting to break through his granite face. Followed by more throat-clearing. "Okay, then. I'd better get back to work. That schooner's going to need a coat of varnish by day's end. Let me put your mother back on the line. Mother, it's Anna!"

As he headed back to the dungeon, I thought I heard whistling, a reminder that Dad was one of the last practitioners of a dying art. Two, if you counted model-ship building.

"I know it's Anna!" my mother yelled after him. "I'm not senile just yet!"

"Never said you were!" he shouted back before shutting the door a little too hard.

Amidst a few crackles and pops initiated by the phone transfer, Mom informed me, "Hi, Anna, it's your mother."

I almost said oy, a word I heard Aaron utter from time to time, but resisted the temptation for fear of opening a new line of discussion. Instead, the exchange continued much as it had before, until I said, "Mom, I gotta run. I need to check on dinner." I knew a brief accounting of my newly developing domestic skills would make her happy. "It was great to talk to you guys. Don't worry about me. Everything's good. Love you."

"Love you, too."

"You should call your aunt."

"I know, Mom. I will."

I hung up fast before someone got weepy. Usually, it was Mom. But lately, I'd had my share of close calls. Of course I should call Auntie. But somehow I found it easier to fib (okay, lie) to my parents than I could to her. She'd always seen right through me.

I knew one of these days I'd have to tell them all what was really going on. But why worry them unnecessarily when I wasn't so sure myself?

CHAPTER 24

I awoke in the blackness of night with a song in my head. It happens more than you'd think. Messages bubbling up from deep in the tar pits of our subconscious, biological emails we block or ignore or tamp down during the day, but that scurry in like termites when the lights go out and our guards come down.

In this instance, the lyric came from the Talking Heads' classic "Once in a Lifetime": "And you may tell yourself/This is not my beautiful house ..."

Just a fragment, but enough to concern me, because later in the song I remembered it says: "My God, what have I done?"

This would require some analysis, because on the surface, at least, I was happy. I loved the baby that grew day by day inside of me, I loved Aaron more than ever, I loved my "beautiful house" that we were bringing back to life with our own four hands (mostly), and I loved the life we were building. So where the heck did the doubt come from?

Sure, I experienced random pangs of homesickness; ironic because, when I left Scandia, I was literally sick of home. But nothing to prompt this.

I stared at the nothingness before me, feeling around the unrumpled sheets on Aaron's side of the bed, a sign he hadn't yet returned from his lounge gig with Meltdown at Bally's. Perhaps the answer was as simple as loneliness (mixed with a dash of isolation)—just the big old house and I still getting to know each other. I chewed on that possibility for a moment as the sounds of the night encroached: a siren, a car horn, a barking dog, a train whistle. Plus, the usual creaks and moans typical of middle-aged structures (and people). A melancholy chorus if ever there was one. I pulled the covers up higher and shuddered.

Could I dare hope for a second round of blessed sleep? The beginning of my second trimester was making it more and more unlikely these days. But as the warmth and oblivion enveloped me, another sound made its presence felt, tiptoeing around the threadbare outer edges of my consciousness. Barely present at first, indistinguishable from a dream, but then muffled, like your parents' murmurs from behind closed doors. It required my absolute concentration to will it into focus, the way you'd adjust the dials on a telescope to bring a distant celestial body into crystalline view. It was as annoying as walking with a grain of sand in your shoe; try as I might, I could not ignore it. So I threw back the blanket and slipped into my robe, cinching it tight at what passed for my waist. Could I have left the TV on before going to bed? I clearly remembered turning it off, although my memory wasn't what it used to be, the growing alien in my tummy stealing my mojo by the day. Stupidly, I flicked on the light and set off to find the source of the babble, not stopping to think it could be burglars or worse.

A downstairs room-to-room inspection yielded nothing. But as I got closer to the stairs (all 17 of them), I noticed a second element added to the mix: the faint, but unmistakably pungent, aroma of cigar smoke.

A smart woman would have called 911. But what would I say? I hear a TV and smell a cigar? Please send your crack SWAT team immediately? Instead, I made my way to the kitchen and grabbed a rubber mallet from the rack, the kind you use to pound chicken into cutlets. I'm sure the sight was laughable: a pregnant woman awkwardly wielding a cooking utensil certain to strike terror in the heart of any home invader.

I stopped to catch my breath on the upstairs landing before completing my ascent and moving methodically down the long hall, poking my head into each room to—what? Assure myself it was all a figment of my overripe imagination? Was that really preferable to an actual intruder?

The hammering of my own heart was the only sound I heard. Just as I decided to return to the ground floor, it started up again, the noise and the stench stronger than before, now punctuated by what sounded like a crowd of people laughing. Peering down the far end of the corridor, I could just make out bluish light spilling out from under the door of the guest room, a 10-by-10 space I'd set foot in only a handful of times before.

Again, I considered bailing, but my natural reporter's curiosity got the better of me and I soldiered on, each step like walking in Jell-O. My puffy feet delivered me to the door nonetheless. Now the sounds were unmistakable: the tenor tones of a man's voice, ethnic, possibly Hispanic; and a woman, whiny and strident, engaged in a hilarious back-and-forth conversation (if the waves of raucous laughter were to be believed). Did this room even have a TV? I couldn't recall.

The door knob felt smooth and cool in my hand. Before I could talk myself out of it, I gave it a turn and pushed. It didn't budge. One last chance to run, or at least shuffle, away. To heck with that. Focusing all my adrenaline and fear and crazy pregnant-lady strength, I put my shoulder into the door like I'd seen in so many cheesy action movies. After a nanosecond pause, it gave way with a thunderous crack!

As my eyes adjusted to the room, they settled on the source of the sounds, a small black-and-white TV with a coat-hanger antenna, the kind I barely remembered from Gramma's house when I was little. (Years later, in my college Marketing 101 class, I learned that Gramma was a "laggard," essentially the last person on the planet to adapt new technology). On the screen, I recognized Lucy and her husband from "Nick at Nite" in mid-quarrel, with Lucy saying, "I may not be able to understand what you say when you say it, but before you say it, I can understand what you're going to say perfectly."

From there, my eyes wandered to a leather recliner on the far side of the room, where an ancient man in equally ancient PJs sat puffing on a stogie the size of a torpedo, the tip glowing an intermittent bright orange, the smoke curling up to the ceiling in the flickering light of the television screen. And, as if the entire scene weren't strange enough already, the man was as ethereal as the smoke, a shimmering silver-gray specter drifting in and out of, well, whatever passed for reality in this room. Not much taller than a jockey, he was sporadically solid enough for me to discern a few features: the head bald, other than a scattering of wispy white hairs, large gnarled hands, and glasses with window-frame lenses held up by ears the size of satellite dishes.

As my raggedy mind tried vainly to process the spectacle, the man or whatever he was turned to me and said in a rusty voice, "I like what you've done with the place."

The rubber mallet made a dull thudding sound as it bounced off the hardwood floor. The scream I heard might have been my own.

CHAPTER 25

"We see this occasionally, especially in first-time pregnancies," the emergency room doctor said. At well over six feet tall and skinny as an afterthought, he crouched over my bed like a praying mantis in scrubs.

Aaron stood in the background, arms folded, a mask of concern darkening his features. I could only imagine how he felt, returning home after his cover band gig to find me nowhere in sight, the frantic room-to-room search through a lot of rooms, the discovery of what must have looked like my body, growing colder by the second, crumpled in a heap on the guest-room floor, an incongruous rubber mallet by my side.

I had little memory of the ambulance ride, other than the siren wail and the scent of rubbing alcohol, which almost, but not entirely, overcame the cigar smoke that still lingered around me, though I seemed to be the only one who smelled it.

"Did anything unusual precipitate your fainting spell?" the doc asked. He wore a rectangular name tag identifying him as Doctor Feelgood, although, much to my relief, a couple of blinks and a quick shake of my head reconfigured it as Felgar.

Anything? How about everything? It had all seemed so real. But now, in the harsh non-healing glare of fluorescent lights, I wasn't so sure. It must have been a dream so lucid it sent me on a sleepwalking expedition through multiple rooms and floors. But even that explanation made me sound like a wackadoodle, triggering visions of jack-booted social workers swooping down from the rooftop *Minority Report*-style to confiscate my baby at the moment of birth, while I spent the rest of my days in Las Vegas' version of Arkham Asylum.

"No," I said.

Dr. Felgar made a notation on my chart, probably something along the lines of "Patient is compulsive liar," and favored me with a kindly smile designed to keep me calm until the authorities arrived. He said, "The good news is the baby's fine. And so are you."

"Thank God," Aaron said, an interesting choice of words from a self-avowed agnostic. And then, "What's the bad news?" Waiting for the other shoe to drop—a Jewish thing, he'd explained to me not long after we met.

"None, really," the doctor said. "I just want your wife to stay home for the next few days. As a precaution. No driving or anything, in the unlikely event she has another ..." He paused briefly to choose the right word, finally settling on "... episode."

I snorted as I remembered the "I Love Lucy"

episode, quickly covering it by blowing my nose in a Kleenex conveniently placed on the tray table in front of me. Aaron and the doctor sent questioning looks my way nonetheless. I would need to be more careful if I wanted to stay out of the rubber room.

"I also want her to make an appointment with her OB/GYN as soon as possible. In the meantime, get plenty of rest, stay hydrated, read a good book. Pretend you're on a little staycation. And no moving around unnecessarily."

Aaron scrutinized me and grinned, the first time I'd seen anything but fear on his face since opening my eyes. "So I'm supposed to wait on you hand and foot?"

"Yep. Doctor's orders." I looked at Dr. Felgar for confirmation, but got only a little nod in return.

"Okay," Aaron said. "But only under protest."

Dr. Felgar looked like he couldn't wait to get out of there. "No reason to keep you here," he said, eyeing the opening in the curtain. "I'll have the nurse prepare the paperwork. You'll be back in the world in no time."

He was a man of his word. Thirty minutes later, we were home, ordinarily the most welcoming place in the world. So why did my blood run cold the moment I walked in the door?

CHAPTER 26

“I’ve made an executive decision,” Aaron said as he laid a plate of oatmeal-raisin cookies and a big glass of milk on the tray in front of me. Per Dr. Felgar, he’d been delivering food and beverages the last two days and even seemed to be getting the hang of it. I knew I was perfectly capable of fending for myself, but why spoil the fun? Actually, other than a tiny bump on the back of my head, I’d never felt better. The creature (girl, dammit!) we’d affectionately dubbed “ET” was finally kicking in with some long-awaited second-trimester mojo that accounted for my neon glow and newfound energy reserves.

“Do tell,” I said with what I pictured as my best bemused expression. Aaron’s “executive decisions” were typically innocuous and inconsequential, ranging from changing dinner plans to insisting on a new brand of toilet paper. But this time he seemed serious, so I paused the Lifetime weepie DVD I’d been watching and gave him my full attention.

"Two decisions, actually. Although they're connected. So it might be One A and One B."

I recognized this as a classic Aaron stalling tactic. "Go on," I encouraged.

He gulped audibly. "I'm going to ask Boozer to move in with us."

"Boozer? Seriously?" I liked him fine, even found him entertaining in an odd way, although I would never tell him that. But that didn't mean I wanted him back as a roommate. Aaron forged ahead like an intrepid jungle explorer with a machete.

"Wait, hear me out. Sure, he's a little nuts ..."

"A lot nuts."

"Okay, I'll grant you that. But he's got retard strength."

Off my pretend appalled look, Aaron added, "His term, not mine. Says it's the name of the new comedy showcase he's working on. Regardless, he can be one scary SOB. Believe me. I saw it myself, up close and personal, when he went through his performance-art phase and pissed off half of Las Vegas. One time he got himself booked into some kind of presentation at Weight Watchers and started riffing on marriage vows. 'Sure, it's easy to commit when you're up there with a church full of well-wishers showering you with love and support. For better or worse? Piece of cake, so to speak.' A sprinkling of uneasy laughs from the audience. 'Sickness and health? Can of corn. Creamed corn.' A few unsure sniggers. He paused to survey the room, waiting for just the right moment to strike. 'But nobody said anything about your BIG FAT ASS!' After a short pause, a dozen or so women rushed the stage and Boozer handled them like Earl Campbell shaking off defenders."

I had no idea who Earl Campbell was, but filed it away while I continued to process the idea of Boozer leaving the toilet seat up and peeing all over the floor and beating off to the Carl's Jr. commercial.

Aaron continued, "And you'll never find a more loyal friend. He'd take a bullet for me. And you."

I could visualize Boozer doing just that. Coupled with Aaron's sincere Boy Scout expression, I simply couldn't say no. "All right," I said after making him squirm just a little too long. "But the first time he leaves his underwear in the middle of the living room floor, he's outta here." I jerked my thumb toward the front door for emphasis.

"Agreed," Aaron said.

I checked to see if his fingers were crossed.

We shook on it, followed by a long kiss to seal the deal.

"What's the second thing?" I asked when we were done.

Aaron's face betrayed confusion.

"The second thing," I repeated. "You know, One B."

"Oh, right," he said. "We're getting a dog."

CHAPTER 27

This would be a good time to mention that research is my superpower. I've always wanted to understand how things happen. And why. It's the reason I became a journalist.

Of course, everyone has access to all the information in the world on the Internet. But too much data can be just as useless as not enough. How do you sort it all out, determine what's legit and what's bogus? Fortunately, through a combination of education, intuition, and DNA, I possess a highly evolved BS detector. Plus, I flat-out enjoy the process. I can get lost in the digital rabbit hole for hours, following leads and loops, sifting through red herrings and false positives, assessing brilliant observations and unfounded beliefs. And the best part is uncovering a nugget of wisdom amidst all the nonsense. That's what makes it worthwhile.

So after googling Earl Campbell ("hard-hitting NFL Hall of Fame power running back for the now-defunct Houston Oilers"), I turned my Web attention to choosing the breed of dog I wanted to welcome into our fast-growing family. This wasn't a decision taken lightly. We needed a protector that was highly intelligent, loyal, fierce, and big enough to take out any intruder with ease, but gentle and patient enough to play with the baby, while putting up with all manner of ear-pulling and eye-gouging indignities. It would also help if he came with a sonic-boom bark and a menacing growl to give even the most hardened henchman the urge to pee.

To take the poochie plunge once again, I also had to get past my own personal history. As a child, I enjoyed a series of canine companions that all came to bad ends. Inviting them into our home was tantamount to a death sentence. Pierre the poodle was a runner; he shot out of even the smallest crack in the front door, until one morning he met up with the business end of a Dodge Caravan. I cried for three days. Newton the Beagle was too smart for his own good; no backyard could hold him and he kept tunneling out like the guy in *The Shawshank Redemption.* But unlike that character, he had a habit of knocking up the neighborhood lassies until the time old Mr. Landfield took the law, and a shotgun, into his own hands. That sobbing jag lasted the weekend. By the time Cookie the mutt died pooping her brains out from a sudden onslaught of parvo (vaccines don't work 100 percent of the time), I had no more tears. And no more desire for another dog.

Still, I knew Aaron was right. When he left for work that night, I made myself a cup of ginger tea, fired up the laptop (stopping briefly to admire the tropical-island screensaver that all Las Vegans seem to fancy), and settled into the most comfortable corner of the sofa, ready to push the envelope to the far reaches of the Webiverse.

First up, "Watchdogs." My initial run-through of credible sources gathered the following results: Akita, Giant Schnauzer, Sheltie, German Shepherd, Chow, Kuvasz, Shar Pei, Doberman, Komondor, Rottweiler, Labrador Retriever, Saint Bernard, Bullmastiff, Boxer. However, many had glaring faults leading to immediate disqualification. Akitas like to stand on their hind legs and give you a big hug, not the most appealing trait for a short girl like me. Giant Schnauzers tend to be overprotective. Shelties run around in circles all day until they make you dizzy. Labs have a big bark and no bite; they'll lick an intruder while he's burgling you blind. Bullmastiffs think they're lap dogs. Boxers fart up a storm. Saint Bernards drool. Chows are insane. Komondors look like mops and require constant untangling. Shar Peis wouldn't scare a kitten. Kuvaszes, well, who could even pronounce it? That left the Shepherd, Doberman, and Rottweiler.

Now a quick cross-reference with "Best Dogs for Kids." While you could make a case for all three, some Dobermans had a tendency to lash out when child's play got too rough. Rottweilers looked imposing, but were "surprisingly gentle," although their sheer size could become a challenge. And German Shepherds deserved their reputation as loyal family protectors willing to put up with a lot. Ultimately, it boiled down to the individual dog, its temperament and disposition. It also depended on how well we taught our girl to develop a healthy respect for animals. I was confident we were up to the task.

And so, armed with this knowledge, Aaron and I drove out the next day with a game plan and the desire to adopt a new pal. Years of exposure to the heart-wrenching Sarah McLachlan ASPCA commercials had conditioned us to avoid the dog breeders and puppy mills at all costs and head instead straight to an animal shelter where we could truly make a difference. In Las Vegas, that meant the Animal Foundation on North Mojave Road.

"Back in the day," Aaron said on the drive over, "this place was like San Quentin—smelly, disease-infested, with every inmate waiting on Death Row. It wasn't unusual to see six or seven dogs stuffed into each cell. My folks took me here when I was a kid and I bawled so much we never did pick out a pup. Luckily, I hear it's changed. Public pressure and all that."

I blanched and said, "Thank God. I don't think I could handle it."

He swung the car into the driveway, parking in a spot not far from the main building, a sprawling low-slung structure painted in the same desert-friendly colors they must give away for free out here. A pleasant young Hispanic woman named Maria checked us in at the front desk and pointed us toward two outside rows of corrugated metal bungalows flanked by an array of solar panels.

"That's where we keep the dogs," she said.

"About two hundred at the moment, so you should have no trouble finding one you like."

Feeling like a little girl at Cedar Point, the Roller Coaster Capital of the World, we systematically combed through each facility in search of our four-legged forever friend, dutifully jotting down relevant details about dogs that caught our eye and tugged at our souls. As we made the rounds, it occurred to me that dogs, like their human counterparts, are in a position to help or hurt their chances based on the way they market themselves.

Resident canines displaying behavioral issues like biting had been sequestered in a form of solitary confinement, the breeds ranging from Dachshunds to Great Danes. As we infringed on their personal space, the snarling and snapping increased exponentially, letting you know they'd rip your lungs out for a Milk Bone. As a rule, the people showing interest in them looked as mean as the dogs. I found the whole scene depressing and couldn't get out of there fast enough.

In the next building, some of the smaller breeds, Chihuahuas and the like, shook with unremitting anxiety or cowered in the corner. A few managed to wet themselves. We felt sorry for them, but gave them a wide berth. Desperation is never an effective strategy.

In subsequent venues, other dogs ignored us completely, while some appeared too eager: jumping, wagging, and fawning over us like overly attentive waiters.

After more than two hours, we came up empty.

"I'm not feeling it," I said as we exited the final building, not disguising my disappointment.

"There're plenty other places we can try," Aaron said. No sooner had the words left his mouth than a welcoming woof spun me around to discover its source, a sturdy fellow with short wiry white hair, a black circle orbiting one eye, and a big grin splashed across his face.

"He likes you," said the tall heavily tatted blonde girl holding one end of his leash. "We just came back from his walk and he pulled me over here with all his might. Which is mighty indeed."

When I bent to pet him, he wagged his whole body and slobbered me like I was drenched in peanut butter.

"What kind of dog is he?" I heard Aaron ask between giggles (mine) and happy whimpers (dog).

"American Staffordshire Terrier," she said.

Aaron's expression turned guarded. "Wait a minute. Isn't that a fancy name for Pit Bull? He looks like one."

"Not exactly. But they are related. Cousins, actually."

Aaron put his foot down. Or at least stomped it. "Absolutely not."

The dog stopped in mid-lick and turned his massive noggin toward Aaron, with me a split second behind.

"But he's such a good boy," I said. The dog stepped up his wagging in a show of support. "How can you say no to those Bambi eyes?"

"I know he seems fine now," Aaron said. "But

those breeds can turn on you in an instant. You've seen the news reports. I wouldn't feel right with him hanging around the baby."

The blonde with the leash jumped in and said, "Those stories are overblown by the media. Plus, it all depends how you treat them. This boy's been here almost three weeks and he's a sweetheart. Not even a growl. His previous owners left him behind when they did the midnight move. A real estate agent found him when she came to take photos. He'd eaten all the cabinets. How people can treat their pets like that is beyond me. The Realtor wanted to keep him, but her husband wouldn't hear of it." She tossed a nasty look in Aaron's direction.

I piled on. "See, he's had a hard life. He'll be so grateful to be with a family who loves him." I could tell Aaron was wavering when the blonde made him an offer he could hardly refuse.

"Why don't you take him home and test him out," she said with her most genuine smile. "If you don't like him for any reason, bring him back. No questions asked."

"That gives us plenty of time to find out," I said. "Besides, you're fine leaving me with Boozer, but not this guy?"

Aaron thought for at least a minute, his face moving through all kinds of contortions before softening ever so slightly. "All right," he said. "But if he so much as looks at me cross-eyed, he's back in jail."

I managed to stand without too much awkwardness and delivered a grateful hug, while our new best friend rolled around on a little patch of grass, making gurgling sounds.

"That's awesome," our benefactor said. "You can go inside to start the paperwork."

"I don't know how to thank you," I said.

"No worries. I'm really happy for you guys." She tried giving me an awkward embrace that disintegrated into a pat on the back.

"I forgot to mention," she called after us as we made our way toward the main building. "His name's Lucky."

CHAPTER 28

I'd gotten in the habit of getting up just before dawn to sit in the courtyard and luxuriate in the coolest part of the day, which lasted all of five minutes and consisted of a mere whisper of a breeze. Most mornings it was just Lucky, me, and the neener-neener bird, a small black fellow with an orange crest splashed proudly across his chest, so christened by me after his singular endless-loop cry. I liked to think of it as some type of mating declaration, and while no suitable companion ever appeared, he would not be dissuaded, hopping around, chest out, as if his feather-mate were just around the corner. I admired his tenacity in the face of harsh reality.

On this particular morning, I brought along my laptop to indulge in some serious investigation, not on behalf of my PBS employer, but for my own peace of mind.

Now that the dust had settled on my fainting spell (dust, in fact, is something we have in abundance here in southern Nevada, along with grit, sand, soot, and smut), I couldn't stop thinking about my vision of the old man with the cigar. The whole episode had seemed so real, in some ways more so than my day-to-day existence. If it was a dream, it was the most lucid one I'd ever experienced. Revisiting the upstairs guest bedroom did no good; except for a twin bed and some assorted boxes, it was empty. If my visitor had been an actual spirit, he'd conjured up the whole tableau.

The previous afternoon, I'd casually (I hoped) asked Aaron if he believed in ghosts. Instead of answering outright, he responded with a question of his own, as is his way.

"Why do you ask?"

"I don't know. I hear creaks and groans coming from the house all the time. Don't you?"

He set aside the guitar he'd been noodling around on to focus on my inquiry. At length, he said, "Never noticed. But it's not surprising. That's what old houses do."

"I know. But sometimes they sound so ... human."

"Trick of the mind," he said and I knew that was the end of this line of questioning. So I was on my own.

My first key-phrase foray, "Haunted Places in Las Vegas," yielded no meaningful results, although it did pique my interest in the Boulder Dam Hotel, purportedly the home of much paranormal activity.

Narrowing my search to "Las Vegas Haunted Houses" was a complete waste of time, delivering page after page of commercial enterprises with names like "Gates of Hell," "Voodoo Village," and

"Asylum," the kinds of places that pop up out of the desert weeks before Halloween and disappear just as fast.

I changed tacks on my third try, attempting to track historical ownership of the house. Duh! Why didn't I start with this? I chalked it up to baby brain.

We'd purchased the house directly from Independence Mortgage; prior to that, according to a local business weekly, it had been owned by an LLC that had attempted, and failed, to get a zoning variance for a pre-school and subsequently went belly up. Too bad. With all the rooms, it could have accommodated something like a hundred kids.

The pre-school company had bought it from a private individual, but that's where the trail went cold, at least momentarily, until I stumbled onto the Clark County Recorder's Office. A well-placed click on "Search Records" had me scrambling for our parcel number. That, after input, led me straight to—bingo!—Deeds of Trust, where I traced what they called the "chain of title" back to the first owner, one Meyer Levin, who'd purchased the original parcel of land in 1959.

Rather than some obscure Las Vegas nobody, Meyer Levin turned out to be a rather big deal, even occupying his own Wikipedia page. My breathing came in short gasps as I pored over the entry, discovering that Levin was a Prohibition-era bootlegger-turned-Las Vegas casino owner and philanthropist, a scion of the community who vanished like smoke in 1988.

While no photograph accompanied the entry,

I knew I was only a click or two away. And there, in article after article in all the city's daily, weekly, and monthly publications, stared the same image of a rough-hewn elderly man with thick glasses, wispy white hair, and oversized ears jutting out like stop signs on a school bus.

"Hello, Meyer," I said when I managed to catch my breath. "Welcome home."

CHAPTER 29

The letter came on a Tuesday, registered, signature required, courtesy of our sourpuss shorts-clad carrier who looked like he was mere weeks away from hanging up his pouch for good. The letter caught me by surprise, because nothing of importance ever came on a Tuesday. As I autographed the receipt, our postman craned his neck in an obvious attempt to see past the foyer into the house, no doubt curious about the remodel.

"You're welcome to come in and have a look around," I said in my friendliest Midwestern tone.

Instead of taking me up on my offer, or even acknowledging it, he turned on his heels and high-tailed it back to the safety of his truck. I filed away a mental image for the time I'd see him online or on CNN, being led off in handcuffs after shooting up our neighborhood p.o.

The letter was from Pyke's Peak Corporation and got straight to the point. Due to the casino-hotel's "pressing need" to expand its parking capacity, they were prepared to tender a very generous offer for our property, considerably more than the appraised value. They were certain we'd have questions, so they'd scheduled a series of informal meetings to address our concerns, quash unfounded rumors, and generally provide assurances as to the seriousness of their intentions.

There was more, but I was finding it increasingly difficult to focus, between my wildly beating heart and the inability to catch my breath.

"Fuck you," I somehow choked out to the faceless attorney whose name was on the letter, a phrase I had uttered only a handful of times in my life. "This house is not for sale."

CHAPTER 30

With a hot psychotic wind whipping through the valley and Aaron still sleeping off the previous night's gig, I used my limited graphic skills to design a 10-point manifesto explaining in simple WIIFM ("What's in It for Me") terms why the neighbors should all band together and hold out against turning our fine old street into a parking lot. I was hoping to find plenty of people home at this hour on a Saturday morning, but if not, I'd leave a flyer inviting them over for coffee where we could discuss our ideas in a sensible non-emotional manner. Feeling like a rookie candidate running for City Council, I set off with a combination of fear, excitement, and determination to make my case one house at a time.

I came up empty on my first three attempts—a relief, if I'm being honest. Rolling up the flyers into tight scrolls, I used two rubber bands each to secure them to the door knobs. The last thing I needed was to have a big gust scatter them around the block, not the best way to ingratiate myself to the neighbors. At the fourth house, a

Spanish-style structure with a red mission-tile roof, circular drive, and an actual patch of semi-green grass in front, my knocking triggered a hyper response from a yappy dog (and not much else). I was about to roll up another flyer when a crone-like rasp called out, "Hold your horses! I'm coming! I'm coming!" Minutes later, after the metal-on-metal rattle of latches unlatching and chains unclasping, a dreadfully bony old woman in a stained off-white housecoat and bunny slippers to match scowled at me over her glasses and said, "You're that new one."

How she could possibly know was anyone's guess, unless she spent her days at the window spying on us through 50X magnification. The thought made me shudder, but I carried on, the opportunity to deliver my first spiel bringing my thoughts into focus.

"Yes, ma'am," I said, handing her a flyer while unveiling my most sincere smile. "I was wondering if I could talk to you about the letter from Bob Pykowski. You got one, right?"

"We all did. But save your breath, young lady. I think it's the best idea since sliced bread. So does Gladys Mason and Nancy Petrocelli and Maria Cabrera and the rest of the widows living hand-to-mouth on our husbands' social and the tips we pick up watching 'Extreme Couponing.' Pykowski's a strange bird, but God bless him. We thought we were stuck here, but now there's an escape clause, so you run along and thank your lucky stars you don't have to spend the rest of your life on this shithole street." Her ugly little dog grunted in agreement as she slammed the door in my face, leaving me sputtering on her doorstep.

Well, no one said it would be easy. Once I got myself under control, I continued up the street, purposely avoiding the residences whose mailboxes specified Mason and Petrocelli and Cabrera, figuring I'd be wasting my breath. Finally, toward the end of the block, I saw a tall older gentleman, thin as an exclamation point, somehow managing to keep his military cap from falling off while he stooped to retrieve the newspaper in his driveway.

"Excuse me, sir," I said with what I hoped was a friendly wave. "May I take just a few moments of your time?" And steeled myself for the certain rejection to come. Is this what professional salespeople dealt with every day? How long would it take to crush my soul flat as a shadow?

To my surprise, he returned my smile with one of his own, saying, "Of course. What can I do you for?"

I extended my hand and said, "My name is Anna Eisenberg. Your new neighbor from across the street."

His handshake was firm but not overpowering. "Charles T. 'Chuck' Caldwell, Captain, USMC, retired. You and your husband did a nice job of fixing up that old dump. Meyer's place."

"Thank you. Did you know Meyer?" Veering off topic, but too curious to miss a genuine opportunity.

"I did. Nice old gentleman, quiet, kept to himself. Except for when he threw these lavish parties for his business associates, big-money guys. One time he invited the missus and me, and we met Wayne Newton. Never liked the guy myself, thought he sang like a girl. But Gina, God rest her soul, was over the moon. And Newton was nice as could be. Anyway, Meyer was an ideal neighbor. We heard the rumors, of course, but never saw any evidence of it. Not a hint."

"Rumors?"

"Yes. That he was a stone-cold killer."

I shivered although the temperature easily topped 100 degrees.

"Sorry, I guess I derailed the conversation," he said, looking me up and down in a non-creepy way. "You're too old to be selling Girl Scout cookies. So my guess is you want to talk about that son-of-a-bitch Pykowski and his horseshit offer. Well, let's go inside, so we can plot against the whites."

As I followed him into his home, the pleasant aroma of bacon and coffee made my mouth water, all the more so because both items placed high on the pregnant woman's verboten list.

Perhaps sensing my disappointment, Mr. Caldwell said, "I'd offer you a cup of coffee, but I'm not sure it's appropriate for a woman in your delicate condition." He paused while a look of consternation crossed his face. "Unless, of course, you're not, in which case I've really stepped in it, which I've been known to do."

I assured him that his assessment was one hundred percent accurate and asked for a glass of water instead, which he delivered in a San Diego

Chargers tumbler. As he read my flyer, I tried to inconspicuously eyeball his living room, where a whole school of stuffed fish and deep-sea fishing photos adorned every square inch of dark-wood paneling that didn't display pictures of Chuck in various military uniforms. Although impeccably maintained, the room was utterly devoid of a woman's touch.

"You're a good writer," he said, interrupting my musings.

"Thank you," I said. My old self would have knee-jerked some type of "aw shucks, who me?" comeback, but the new one had been working on accepting compliments graciously. Not that I got too many, but I left it at that. Besides, I was. A good writer.

"I especially like number six: 'Don't let the bastards win.' You're one feisty filly."

"It's a recent development."

"You've probably figured out by now the rest of our neighbors are going to be of no help whatsoever. A bunch of greedy dried-up old biddies who don't give a rat's patoot about anyone but themselves."

I nodded in agreement, finishing the last swallow of water. "So what do we do?"

"There's a meeting next Saturday, week from today. Did you get the notice?"

"Not yet."

He handed me a professional circular that looked like it came from a top marketing firm. "You have now. I plan to get there early, reconnoiter, see if we have any other allies in this slog. I doubt it, but it never hurts to find out. Either way, I'm in it for the duration. After Khe Sanh, this is a walk in the park. At least nobody dies."

He stopped to consider this last statement. "Although I wouldn't put it past 'em."

CHAPTER 31

They held the meeting at the Landmark Presbyterian Church on East Oakey Blvd., just around the corner from our house. Las Vegas, I'd heard, has more churches per capita than most U.S. cities. The standing joke is that we need them. Nothing in the previous months had convinced me otherwise.

I'd been nervous about this meeting ever since Mr. Caldwell showed me the notice. In my mind, it represented a final chance for our community to draw a line in the sand. But could we be characterized as a "community" at all? Or just a bunch of strangers looking out for themselves? My door-to-door initiative had provided more than a clue. And tonight would probably answer the question once and for all.

Aaron and I arrived at the domed, two-story, white-cinderblock structure fifteen minutes early. (According to Aaron, the building possessed multiple personalities; it had, at various times, housed the Sikhs, the Jehovah's Witnesses, and even the

Masons). I'd wanted to get there even earlier, but couldn't stop messing with my hair and makeup and trying on different outfits before settling on a basic-black maternity pantsuit that (I hoped) made me look competent and professional. If I had to get up and make a speech, it would be nice to be taken seriously. Aaron stood around tapping his foot and glancing at his watch every two minutes, but didn't say a word, for which I was grateful.

The main assembly hall held roughly 200 people and was already two-thirds full, most of them engaged in a buzz of animated conversation. Swiveling my head from left to right and back again, I scanned the room for a friendly face before stopping on the trademark Marines First Calvary Division olive-drab ball cap seemingly glued to the bald pate of Mr. Caldwell. A little wave of relief washed over me. No matter what happened, Aaron and I wouldn't be the sole holdouts. I took Aaron's hand and led him to where Mr. Caldwell was camped out.

"Anna!" he said, blanketing me in a fatherly hug and motioning toward a couple of metal folding chairs. "I saved you and your husband a seat." He stuck out a bony hand in Aaron's direction and they shook. "Chuck Caldwell. Happy to finally meet you."

"Same here, sir," Aaron said. "Anna speaks very highly of you."

Mr. Caldwell waved off the compliment. "Don't put too much stock in it. Anna speaks highly of everybody. Even you." He gave me a wink.

Aaron chuckled. "You think she'd have caught

on to me by now. But it's just her way."

"I hope this town doesn't ruin her." Suddenly serious.

"You and me both."

I gesticulated wildly. "Hey guys, I'm right here. And I'm tougher than I look."

"You might have to be," Mr. Caldwell said in an ominous tone.

Before the conversation could make me any more uncomfortable, a jowly older man wearing a crisp white shirt—with epaulets, no less—and matching yachting cap lumbered to the podium mic, tapping on it three times. The thump-thump-thump silenced the room. "Is this thing on?" he asked. "Testing one, two. Testing one, two. Check, check."

"It's on, Harry!" a voice yelled from the back of the room. "Give it a rest! You never asked for a check in your life!"

"Yeah!" bellowed another. "You act like you've never seen a microphone before. It looks like your wife's you-know-what!" The crowd shouted the second heckler down and he quickly retreated to the relative safety of his chair.

The man they called Harry ignored them both. "Okay, please take your seats. Let's get this program started. We have important business to discuss." He took a sip from a Super Big Gulp, stifled a burp, and continued, "I'm Harry Brown, president of the Oakmont Estates Neighborhood Association."

Mr. Caldwell leaned over and whispered in my ear, "What a bunch of happy horseshit, pardon my language. They just made up that highfalutin' name so they could get their hands on more money."

Brown went on, "It's nice to see so many of our friends and neighbors here tonight. As you know, the attorneys representing Pyke's Peak Casino, Hotel and Tower have made what I feel is a generous offer to purchase our homes and property to make way for an expansion project that will put a significant amount of cash in our pockets and add construction jobs to our community at a time when we desperately need to put people back to work." He stopped and cleared his throat, looking pleased with himself.

A murmur swept through the audience and I could see people nodding their heads in agreement. Mr. Caldwell leaned in again. "So much for having an impartial moderator." Aaron squeezed my hand in support, but it did little to quell my uneasy feelings.

"But enough of my ramblings," Brown said. "I'm delighted to introduce Mr. Philip Parkinson, Chief Operating Officer for the Pyke's Peak Holding Company and personal liaison to Mr. Pykowski himself. Mr. Parkinson will make a brief opening statement and will then field your questions."

Philip Parkinson, tall, mid-fifties, perfect posture, $200 haircut, tanning-bed bronze, and impeccably attired in an expensive blue blazer, khakis, and alligator loafers, no socks, strode easily to the podium and gave Brown the two-handed politician's handshake before dismissing him. Surveying the room, Parkinson smiled, showing a mouthful of impossibly white teeth that reminded me of piano keys.

"Pykowski's personal hatchet man, named after a disease. Besides Pykowski himself, one of the most hated men in Las Vegas. And that's saying a lot," Mr. Caldwell said, not bothering to whisper this time. A rotund lady with a marionette face spun around and threw him a disapproving glare.

"I am so pleased to be here tonight," Parkinson said, his voice rich and commanding with just a hint of twang. "Mr. Pykowski expresses his deepest regrets at not being able to appear in person, but he's on a business trip in Macau and couldn't return in time. Please know, however, that he sincerely believes a successful outcome is in the best interest of everyone concerned. In his words, he simply wants everyone to 'get happy.'"

"Mainly himself," Mr. Caldwell said and the old lady shushed him this time.

"I wasn't born and raised in Las Vegas," Parkinson continued. "Most of us hail from somewhere else. But when I moved here from Kansas City more than three decades ago, I immediately fell in love with this town—the people, the confidence, the opportunities. Las Vegas is truly the last bastion of rugged individualism and bootstrap values, a land where you can still grab your piece of the American Dream. Even during the last difficult years. And now we're on the road to prosperity once again, a little older, a little wiser perhaps. Proving that you can't keep good folks down. That's why I'm here today. To offer you a genuine opportunity, one that probably won't present itself again in your lifetimes. In the spirit of fairness, we have retained the services of Walter Bleak and Associates, the most respected appraisal service in southern Nevada, to provide an objective and honest assessment of your property values based on today's prevailing economic conditions. But we didn't stop there ..."

"He sounds like an infomercial," Mr. Caldwell said and shushed himself this time, beating the old woman to the punch. Her contemptuous scowl could no doubt be seen from the International Space Station.

"... a full twenty percent above market value ..."

Assorted oohs and aahs from the crowd, causing the sinking feeling in my stomach to settle somewhere below knee-level.

"We know how much your homes mean to you. You've made lives for yourselves, raised your families, and created lasting memories. We understand that no amount of money can replace those cherished moments. But we hope that our generous good-faith offer will go a long way toward easing your transition as you begin the next chapter of this adventure we call life."

The room burst into spontaneous applause. All except for the three of us, a small island of negative body language sitting with arms folded and looking like we just bit into olive pits.

"We're fucked," is all Mr. Caldwell could murmur, followed by the obligatory, "pardon my French." Glancing at Aaron, I could see he agreed.

"And now I'll open the floor to questions, comments, and concerns." Parkinson's smile radiated practiced sincerity.

"Where do we sign?" The voice came from somewhere behind me and was greeted by good-natured laughter.

"Yeah, I hope you brought enough pens!" More yucks.

"Rest assured," said Parkinson, rubbing his hands together vigorously. "Anyone else?"

Mr. Caldwell struggled to his feet. "Well, here goes nothing," he muttered before addressing the crowd. "I'm Chuck Caldwell. You know me. I've lived in this neighborhood since before many of you were born. I served my country with pride, did two tours in Nam, bought this house on the GI Bill. My kids went to school alongside yours, right up the street at Bishop Gorman. My wife Gina and I lived here happily our entire marriage until she passed almost two years ago. May she rest in peace." He stopped to clear his throat and I could see some mistiness around his eyes. "I'm sixty-eight years old, I got a bum ticker and hips to match, and my next move is going to be Woodlawn," he harrumphed with finality.

"That's a cemetery," Aaron whispered in my ear.

Appropriate, because the room had grown deathly silent. Mr. Caldwell eased himself back into his seat, his expression grim.

"All right then," Parkinson exhaled. "I must remind everyone that ours is an all-or-nothing proposition. In other words, if even one individual votes no, the properties become worthless to us and the transaction is dead in the water. So the rest of you may want to engage in a neighborly conversation with the General here and help him see the error of his ways. Any other dissenting opinions or is our friend an army of one?"

"I'm a Marine, you horse's ass!" Mr. Caldwell yelled. "Captain Charles T. Caldwell, retired."

"My apologies," Parkinson said. "Thank you for your service. I didn't mean to offend."

I shot up out of my chair before I could talk myself out of it. "I have something to say." Geez, I sounded like a 12-year-old. All heads in the room snapped toward me in unison. I clenched my fists to keep my hands from shaking.

"And you are?" Parkinson asked.

"Anna Eisenberg." I still liked the sound of that.

"Okay Miss Eisenberg ..."

"Mrs." I liked the sound of that, too.

"Mrs. Eisenberg. What do you have to say?"

I drew a breath and coughed. My mouth felt like Death Valley and I wished I'd brought a water bottle. But it was too late now.

"My husband and I have lived on St. Louis only a short time. But we've poured our hearts and souls into our place, turned it into a real home. I can honestly say I love it. I love this whole neighborhood. It has charm and character. When I imagine our future and raising our family together, I picture us right here. That's my dream. How can you possibly put a price tag on something like that?"

I sat down, still trembling. Aaron patted my leg supportively. Mr. Caldwell gave me a thumbs-up.

Other than that, crickets. So much for a future career in politics.

The old lady who had been staring daggers at Mr. Caldwell got to her feet. "In my experience, when people say it's not about the money, it's about the money. Sweetie, how can you even think about blowing this deal for a few extra bucks? That's just about the most selfish thing I've ever heard. Don't ruin it for the rest of us, just because you're looking for a bigger payday."

By their reaction, the crowd clearly agreed. My face flushed, but I held my tongue.

A weather-beaten middle-aged man with an Eastern European accent chimed in. "Young lady, with all due respect ..." I've noticed that when people say that, whatever follows is never good. Or even respectful. I braced myself for the rest. "... You have no right to hold us up for hostage. We have worked hard, paid out our dues. It is time we get big rewarded for our efforts. And we're not going to let some carpet-bomber ..."

"Carpetbagger," someone corrected.

"What I said. Carpet-blogger come into our neighborhood and tell us what to do. And Caldwell, you should be ashamed of yourself, too."

"Oh, you're real brave now, Farkas," Mr. Caldwell snapped back. "Why don't I pay you a visit later tonight and we'll see how brave you are, you Albanian piece of ..." He attempted to rise, but Aaron stopped him with a restraining hand.

"You don't scare me mister old-time man, with your stupid hat you probably bought at the Salvation Army and your ..."

Parkinson intervened. “Order! Order! Let’s return to the business at hand. Are there any other comments?”

There were, all in the same vein. We sat there and took it, because we knew we weren’t going to change anyone’s mind. And they weren’t going to change ours. Our only goal was to get out of there in one piece and live to fight another day.

We also knew this was just a taste of things to come.

CHAPTER 32

"Have you heard the expression 'You can't fight city hall'?" Marty Rosen stifled a yawn, his eyes watering from the effort.

We were sitting in his office in what amounted to not much more than an executive suite on Sunset and effing Eastern. It was the kind of office that had a shared receptionist who fielded every phone call like it came from a salesperson. Aaron had been right; the drive over had been a nightmare, what with all the lane closings and enough traffic to make it look like the rapture in reverse.

Sensing something important, I reached in my purse for a pen and pad, somehow disturbing the X-rated flyer I'd been handed so many months before, causing it to fall onto Rosen's desk practically in front of him. Mortified beyond belief, I scooped it back up while he kept talking as if nothing had happened, confirming my suspicion that he was used to seeing much worse.

"Well," he continued, "Pykowski owns city hall. Or at least a piece of it." A smallish forty-something man with birdlike movements and a rat-atat vocal delivery, Rosen rocked back and forth in his executive chair two sizes too big and awaited our response.

"What do you mean?" we said almost in unison.

"The mayor, the City Council, all bought and paid for with campaign contributions, some aboveboard, some not. You're going up against a juggernaut, one that will steamroll over you, your house, and your dreams, and leave them as barren as this godforsaken litterbox we've chosen to live in for reasons better left to a shrink. There's one next door, if you're interested. A shrink, I mean. Not a litterbox. Here's my free advice. Take the deal, just like your neighbors. I'm not in the habit of turning away business, but you can't win this. And you'll spend a fortune trying."

His bright green eyes took on the look of a small rodent as they darted back and forth between us, while I snuck another peek at the diploma dangling precariously on the wall. Aaron and I had made a dozen or more calls to attorneys with no success. Rosen was the only one who would even talk to us. And he offered a free consultation. At least he was living up to the slogan prominently displayed on his home page: "When you hire Rosen, you get Rosen." Not much of a stretch, considering he was a one-man show.

"I can leave you kids to talk about it if you'd like," he said, rising from his chair.

I remembered my father's words of advice, "If you retain a professional, it pays to listen to him." But I could tell from Aaron's expression he wasn't ready to throw in the towel just yet. And neither was I. "No, we're good," he said.

Rosen smiled and riffled through a stack of papers. They made a thwap sound as he straightened them against his desk.

"You seem like a nice young couple, a growing family ..." he continued, focusing on my expanding belly. "I'm pleased I could help you save some money and headaches." He plucked a business card from a plastic desktop holder. "If you ever need something a little more routine—fix a ticket, review a contract ..." He acknowledged my baby bump again. "... draft a will, Rosen's your man."

Aaron shook his head. "Sorry, what I mean is we understand. But I've got more questions. And I know Anna does, too."

Rosen's smile vanished as quickly as it had appeared and now he just looked weary as he fell back in his chair, deflated. Glancing at his watch, he said "Okay, you still have twenty minutes left on your no-cost no-obligation consultation. I want you leaving here saying Marty Rosen is the last of the honest lawyers. So fire away."

"Mind if I take the first stab?" Aaron asked me.

"Not at all." Seeing him in take-charge mode made me feel warm and protected, as though we were a team that always had each other's backs.

He inhaled, held it a few seconds, and said, "Pykowski's not the government. So how can he force us to sell?"

Rosen looked at me and said, "You've got a sharp young fella." Then, "The short answer is, technically, he can't. But he can make your lives a living hell. First, he, or more accurately, those prick—uh, thugs he calls his legal team, will isolate you from your neighbors. They'll tell everyone it's an all-or-nothing deal and you're the only ones standing in the way of them cashing out with a tidy profit. That makes you the bad guys. The pressure will be relentless. Especially because you're the new kids on the block."

He paused to admire his pop-culture reference, oblivious that the expiration date had long since passed.

Rosen continued, "Got any allies in this fight? And make no mistake, it is a fight. A nasty knock-down winner-take-all brawl, actually."

"Just Mr. Caldwell," Aaron said. "A nice old man who lives across the street. Vietnam vet, been there forever. He's not going anywhere."

Rosen said, "So just the two houses." Not a question, a statement of fact.

"I'm afraid so," I said.

"Here's what you can expect. And it will happen fast. Pykowski has the newspaper in his back pocket, especially now that it's more casino-friendly than ever. So you'll see a story in our local rag that paints you and Mr., uh, Caldwell, is it ...?"

We nodded.

"... Mr. Caldwell as greedy money-grubbers standing in the way of progress. That's the opening salvo. Then he'll pay a construction company under the table to start sending dump trucks and earth movers down your street all hours of the day and night. It'll sound like you're living in Baghdad during the invasion. If that's not enough, they'll put up barricades limiting ingress and egress to your own home. You'll be essentially landlocked."

He paused to let the seriousness of the situation sink in. And sink it did, along with my hopes.

"Want more?"

"Yes," I said. It sounded like a squeak.

"At this point, he'll change the rules and buy everyone else out, even Mr. Caldwell if he's had enough. Then he'll cut off the power to all their homes, which includes the swimming pools. Without filters and chemicals, you'll be surprised how fast they'll turn into little swamps, green brackish cesspools that become ideal breeding ground for mosquitos." Off my skeptical expression, he said, "Yes, mosquitos, right here in the desert. You'll need to check and double-check the screens in your house and maybe even surround the baby's crib with netting. How'm I doing so far?"

"Good," I said. "I mean bad. I mean, I don't know." I braced for the other shoe to slam down.

"And then the rats will come."

Boom! I pictured my baby being dragged away by ROUS (Rodents of Unusual Size) from *The Princess Bride* and came this close to screaming. Instead, I took a sip of water and reached for Aaron's hand, as clammy as my own.

Aaron said, "What about the authorities?"

Rosen snorted. "They'll look the other way. Or worse, there's a good chance the cops will be on hand every day to write you up for some imaginary infraction or other. Even if you get 'em all thrown out of court, the time and aggravation will wear you down."

"Unbelievable," I said.

"Shouldn't be," Rosen continued. "Las Vegas is one of the most corrupt cities in America. Somewhere between Chicago and New Orleans, depending on who's doing the ranking. Anyway, if you're still holding out, that's when Pykowski will start playing hardball."

"You mean all that isn't hardball?" Aaron asked.

"Not even close."

Rosen steepled his fingers and paused, letting us to use our imaginations.

When I tired of that, I said, "So you're telling us it's hopeless."

"Pretty much, in my estimation. You do have one play, however. Although it's the longest of shots, like everything else in this town."

It was the first time I'd heard anything approaching optimism since we sat down. "Go on."

"It's an underdog thing, real David and Goliath stuff. Young mother-to-be, loyal newlywed husband, Vietnam vet neighbor ... no, better yet, war hero ..."

"What if he's not?"

"He will be by the time we're done with him."

Rosen said we, and hope flickered like a fluorescent bulb, but I let it pass for now.

He went on, "Let's talk about the house. What'd you say the address was?"

"Three-thirty-nine East St. Louis."

He checked something on his tablet.

"Bingo!" he said at last, his face lighting up. "Vegas is still such a small town. That's Meyer's place. Why didn't you say so?"

I blushed and shrugged, feeling suddenly inadequate. "It didn't occur to me. Does everyone know about our house?"

"Those of a certain age. That old racketeer threw legendary parties. Elvis, the Rat Pack, Johnny Carson all hung out there when they came to town. And the babes!" He gave me an apologetic look. "I guess that's not PC. Anyway, my buddies and I used to sneak in when we were in high school. Sometimes we got thrown out. But sometimes we didn't. If those old walls could talk ..." His voice trailed off into a dreamy reverie. "At any rate, Meyer's place deserves an honored spot in the Register of Historic Places, not bulldozed to make way for some parking lot."

He paused to scribble something down on a sticky and passed it across the desk to me. It contained a name, Ed Scott, along with a phone number and email address.

"Ed's a friend," Rosen explained. "Investigative reporter, ex-Navy Seal, fearless. The closest thing we have to Woodward and Bernstein." I'd learned about the two reporters who broke the Watergate story during the Nixon era in J-School and the attorney seemed pleased when I nodded in recognition. "He's taken on gaming, mining, the Russian mob, Polly's—those slot barns popping up on every corner like melanoma—even his old newspaper. He used to write for them, but they kept watering down his stuff or cutting it altogether, so he jumped ship and went across town to *City Beat*, the alt weekly. Took a big pay cut, but they leave him alone, let him do what he wants. I admire that. When you call him, use my name. If he doesn't hang up right away, he'll help you."

Rosen's intercom beeped and the receptionist announced that his eleven o'clock had arrived a few minutes early. As we stood up and shook hands, Aaron said, "Mr. Rosen, we don't know how to thank you."

The attorney thought for a moment. "If you beat that jackass Pykowski, invite me over for a drink. That'll be thanks enough. And if you don't beat him, invite me over for two."

CHAPTER 33

"I think you've got something here," Ed Scott said, stretching his bulk to its full length, making our couch look like it belonged in a doll house. With his shiny bald head and muscles rippling beneath his white pocket T, he bore an uncanny resemblance to Mr. Clean. Every other newsman I'd ever known sported a pot belly and a mustard stain on his tie, along with that faraway look signaling a three-second delay between the time you asked him a question and the moment his brain engaged. Not Scott. He'd been scrawling furiously in his spiral note pad for the last half-hour, barely pausing to look up, and it made me happy to be in the presence of an old-school reporter. Not only was I thrilled to have him on our side, I was sure I could learn a thing or three from him.

"You were a journalist back east?" he asked. He'd done his homework; that too was evident.

I blushed. "Not a journalist per se. But I did write for our hometown paper, the *Scandia Gazette*. Human-interest mostly."

"Under deadline?"

I nodded.

"They pay you?"

Another nod.

"That makes you a journalist in my book. We can put your skills to good use. I'm leaving on vacation tomorrow. Hawaii. Competing in the Aloha State Triathlon. Before I go, I'll launch a scud in the next edition, just a teaser in my 'Off the Street' column. While I'm gone, I'd like you to work on an LTE."

Aaron frowned. "LTE?"

"Letter to the Editor," I said, patting his arm in what I hoped was a reassuring, not condescending, gesture.

Scott said, "Just recap how you've been picked on so far. Set the context: young couple, newly arrived, starting a family, how you've fallen in love with our community in such a short amount of time. And how you've lovingly restored this historical monument, not that most locals give a rat's ass about that sort of thing, as evidenced by all the great shit we've blown up—Sands, Dunes, and the godawful Landmark, which even I was in favor of. But it couldn't hurt. It only needs to resonate with one or two folks with juice to swing public opinion to your side."

Now it was my turn to frown. "Juice?"

Aaron patted my arm and I had to laugh. "Clout," he said. "It's a Vegas thing."

"Really go for the emotional jugular. You know the drill."

I didn't, not exactly, but I was getting the idea.

As he spoke, Scott stood up and paced the

room. "I'll be back week after next. And then we can really kick this thing into high gear. Just remember, whatever happens, stick to your guns. Pyke's people will lean on you hard, but they cannot force you to sell. They can only try to make you cave."

He studied both of us appraisingly. "I get the feeling you won't. But I need more than a feeling. If we're in this together, I want a guarantee we're riding it to the finish line, no matter what happens."

"Promise," I said.

"Yes, sir," Aaron said.

"My father was 'sir.' Call me Ed."

"Yes, sir. I mean Ed," Aaron said.

Scott reached out a ham hand and we shook. As he took a step toward the door, his eyes landed on Aaron's assemblage of bass guitars, six-strings, keyboards, and other gear.

"I play a little guitar," he said, and I muffled a giggle, thinking how any guitar would look little in Scott's grasp. "Used to be in a group. More of a club, really. We weren't good enough to call ourselves a band. Ink-Stained Wretches. All local reporters. The drummer couldn't keep the beat, the singer couldn't carry a tune, and I only know three chords. Okay, possibly four on a good day, which wasn't that often. Maybe we could jam when I get back. Some Jimi, Stevie Ray. You can do the hard parts ..."

"I'd like that," Aaron said. "And I'd be happy to teach you another chord."

~O~

Ed Scott never made it back. Four days later, Aaron and I were watching TV when the following promo broke in: "Local reporter drowns in Hawaii. News at eleven."

I didn't need to hear any more. The announcement doubled me over like a punch to the solar plexus. Ed Scott was the first person I'd ever met, other than my Uncle Joe, who actually died. I'd only known him for an instant, but it felt like such a loss, not only because he was an ally, but because I genuinely liked the man. No matter what the autopsy showed, I would always believe it was more than an accident.

The tears came hot and bitter. It was then I realized that aloha also means goodbye.

CHAPTER 34

Ed Scott's "Off the Street" column came out on Friday as scheduled, along with a sidebar tribute from the editor and many of Scott's colleagues lamenting the loss of their friend and praising his journalistic courage. True to his word, he'd ended with a teaser, setting the table for a more exhaustive examination that would never come.

"Guess which low-rent casino owner is up to his old tricks, once again putting the big squeeze on young families, war heroes and others unfortunate enough to be living in the shadow of the most embarrassing example of Vegas kitsch since, well, ever? Find out in upcoming columns as we peel back the contaminated curtain to expose corruption, depravity and far worse from the highest levels of government to the subterranean depths of business as usual. See you in a week when I'll be back, tanned, rested and ready to rumble."

My LTE ran as well, basically a recap of our trials to this point that played on the emotional themes we had discussed with Scott and Rosen. For that one issue of *City Beat*, even a casual reader would get the impression that our little battle was the most important in town.

They held the funeral service at Christ the Redeemer Church in Henderson, but I couldn't bring myself to go.

A week later, the Coroner's Office ruled Scott's death an accidental drowning. It made no sense—a man in top physical condition perishing in warm calm seas on a picture-postcard day. I would always believe that somebody got to him, even 3,000 miles away. We, on the other hand, were fewer than three blocks away. Whatever we were messing with just got real serious real fast.

CHAPTER 35

It happened again.

I was starting to think Meyer's visit was a one-time thing until he showed up a few nights later. Aaron was working his lounge gig and Boozer, who'd moved into the upstairs apartment the previous week with the largest duffle bag I'd ever seen, a three-quarter-size Therm-a-Rest backpacking pad, and a set of six pint glasses printed with a diagram of the relative proportions of a Bloody Mary recipe, had gone off to pick up free sliders from a strip club around the block. So Lucky and I were on our own.

Rather than staking out an unused room in a far-off corner of the house, the old ghost just showed up in the kitchen as I was putting the finishing touches on a story about our neighborhood for a blogsite called "Living Las Vegas." He looked a tad younger and a bit more solid than he had the first time around. And all dressed up in a shiny pinstripe suit.

This time I handled the situation with aplomb. Instead of screaming and passing out, I made a conscious decision to treat Meyer like just another interview subject.

"You found my dog," he said randomly.

Lucky, who'd been lying at my feet, perked up his ears and tilted his head in Meyer's general vicinity.

I said, "With all due respect, Meyer, I don't think this is your dog."

"He's my dog, all right. Most definitely. Aren't you, Lucky?"

Lucky yipped as if to say "End of discussion," and would have jumped all over him if he'd actually been corporeal. Still, his response had to be more than a coincidence. With his super-sensitive hearing, perhaps he was tuning into a frequency only animals—and I—could perceive. I'd given up trying to figure it out. All of us were players in a drama (or was it a dark comedy?) that made no sense. Logic and rational thought were of no use to us now. The only meaningful approach was to suspend judgment, be patient, and wait to see how it played out. When you stopped to think about it, the whole scenario was a metaphor for life itself.

"You're right," I conceded. "I was very blessed to find him. He's going to keep an eye on us, that's for sure." I had to admit, I felt much safer with Lucky around. And he was just about the happiest pet in the world, off Death Row, out of his cage, huge house an adequate domain for a dog his size, well-fed and loved, and, it now seemed, actually reincarnated. It couldn't get any stranger—till I tore my eyes off Lucky and they landed right back on Meyer.

"Hey, do you have time for an interview?" Casual, like talking to a Scandia mother about her daughter's first-place finish in the local spelling bee.

Meyer leaned against the wall. Or maybe the wall leaned against him. Regardless, he said, "Nothing but."

"I read about you on the Internet."

"The what?"

"Internet. It's like the world's largest encyclopedia."

He looked pleased. "So I'm in the encyclopedia now. How about that?"

"But I'd rather hear directly from you. To set the record straight." I reached in my purse, pulled out the Olympus digital recorder that had served me so well in my previous life, and clicked it on.

"I never killed anyone, if that's what you mean," Meyer said as if reading my mind. "Never even did any time to speak of. Tell you what. Listen to my story and you be the judge.

"My parents, Moshe and Rose, were born in the 1870s in Belarudka, a small shtetl in Eastern Ukraine that had the misfortune of being situated not far from the Russian border. They knew each other as children and grew up together; my suspicion is they were cousins caught up in an arranged marriage, but I never was able to confirm that with my relations. Regardless, I tend to believe it, because two of my siblings died as toddlers before I was born. I heard years later it was from Tay-Sachs disease, a Jewish genetic disorder that kept the little ones from walking or even sitting up properly. No doubt the result of too much in-breeding.

"Even so, I had two surviving older brothers, Nathan and Samuel, and one older sister, Fanny, who were relatively healthy, although you wouldn't know it from the kvetching that went on, all manner of minor complaints that turned every pain into a cancer and every headache into a stroke. As for me, I had my share of ailments, bow legs and flat feet that hurt like hell my whole life, but I never went on and on about it.

"Anyways, in the early 1900s, the pogroms, anti-Jewish riots, forced my family to immigrate to the United States. Wherever Jews live, it's always the same old song and dance. My guess is it's because of that bum rap we got as Christ-killers. First of all, we didn't crucify him, the Romans did. Second, even if we'd personally hammered in the nails, weren't we just fulfilling Biblical prophecy? No dead Jesus, no resurrection, no Christianity. The goyim never thought it through. It might also have something to do with that whole God's-chosen-people story. That just pisses off the unchosen. Maybe what we've really needed all these years is a good PR firm.

"So my family scraped up enough dough to board a large steamship sailing out of Constanta, Romania, and spent twelve days throwing up in steerage until they reached America, the land of opportunity. For some reason, they sailed into Norfolk, Virginia, not Ellis Island, and on that one detail, I'm here to tell ya, the course of entire generations changed. After getting processed and having the family name shortened from Leibowitz to Levin, they got wind of work in Detroit and made the trek by train with their last remaining cash. Can you imagine this ragtag family arriving in a strange city, tired and broke, not speaking the language, with no place to live and no job prospects, in the dead of winter? Maybe the snow and gloom were a good thing; it probably reminded them of home.

"Back in Belarudka, my father was a coal miner. But mining jobs were in short supply in Detroit, so he started his own business as a junkman. It was at the beginning of the automobile industry and the streets were lined, not with gold, but scrap metal, which brought a pretty penny. It was damned hard work. I should know, because I often rode along with him during the summer as he made his rounds. Cars were arriving on the scene in greater numbers, though my father insisted on clinging to the old ways, with a little *mishegas* thrown in. That's why he drove a buggy pulled by blind horses named Maggie—they were always named Maggie and he preferred blind horses, because he said they were easier to control. I can still hear the clap-clap of Maggie's hooves on the old cobblestone streets as we wound our way through the neighborhood. Funny, in one lifetime, I went from horse-drawn transportation to seeing a man set foot on the moon.

"We didn't have much of a relationship, my father and me. He made it clear I was there to help with the heavy lifting, not to *hok a chainik*, as he said, which means to talk nonsense. Whether it was on the job or at the dinner table, I was to be seen and not heard. The few times I ventured a comment or opinion or even news of the day, he slammed his palm down with a thunderous thwack and shouted, "Sha!" in a booming bass voice that made my mother and me flinch. My parents mainly spoke Yiddish at home, although my father picked up English real fast, probably because it helped in his business. But Ma, who didn't get out much, never had the same opportunity and really butchered the language until the day she died in 1961, well into her eighties.

"Speaking of Ma, she was a terrible cook. She fried up everything in cast-iron skillets, which went along with my father's cast-iron stomach, burning everything beyond recognition. Steak, liver, chicken, it didn't matter. By the time she was done, it all looked and tasted like old shoes and filled the kitchen with a thin layer of greasy smoke. I'm sure I was covered with it, too. But when everyone and everything smells the same, you don't notice so much.

"Looking back, it's clear my parents knew nothing about raising children. Maybe that's why my older brothers got the hell out as soon as they could. Sam married early and started a family and a commercial real estate business out in Los Angeles. He always had the gift of gab, quick with a smile and a funny story. Of course, it didn't really blossom till he got out of my father's house, and he prospered right along with his adopted city.

"Nate phonied up some papers and joined the Navy at sixteen. He saw a lot of action in World

War I as a mate on a destroyer in the North Atlantic, protecting the coast of Ireland from U-boat attacks. The ship he served on, the *USS Jacob Jones*, was sunk by torpedoes and Nate barely made it into a life boat in one piece before the depth charges on the ship all blew, which left him with a permanent limp. He didn't like to talk about it, but I badgered him all the time when I was a kid and finally wore him down.

"By the time I came along in 1909, the only one still at home was Fanny, four years my senior. I might have been an accident; my parents were already in their late thirties. But Fanny was a real piece of work, always causing trouble just for the helluvit. When we walked home from school, if she saw a group of coloreds, she yelled at the top of her lungs, 'God damned shvartzes!' and we'd have to hightail it out of there as fast as our legs would carry us, Fanny pulling my arm so hard it felt like it would come out of the socket. One time they caught us and pummeled her good, although she gave as good as she got. They took it easy on me, because I was still little, so all I had to show for it was a black eye, busted glasses (which Ma taped up), and a loose tooth.

"While I'm on the subject of teeth, it's amazing I kept them my entire life. I never went to a dentist, never owned a toothbrush until I was 13 and my Uncle Norman, my father's brother, gave me one for my bar mitzvah. He had to show me how to use it, too.

"We lived in a two-story red-brick duplex on Hastings Street on the lower east side, a stone's throw from the Detroit River. It was a poor neighborhood, packed with Jews and Italians and Greeks and coloreds living shoulder to shoulder, but we all got along okay (when Fanny wasn't stirring up trouble). Today, it would be called a slum or a ghetto, but back then we didn't know the kind of bad shape we were in, because we were all in it together.

"We had a dog, Lucky, a feisty black-and-white Bull Terrier like the one in the 'Our Gang' comedies. This dog right here," he said, pointing. Lucky whimpered at mention of his name. "He was a good boy when he wasn't knocking over the trash or munching on my only pair of shoes, which Ma had slipped cardboard cutouts into to cover the holes. Lucky just showed up one day and hung around until we took him in. My mother wouldn't hear of it, but for some reason my father took a liking to him right off the bat, maybe because he never made a sound. Never once heard him bark. The old man had a soft spot for that mutt and the feeling was mutual, the only time I saw my father in a light-hearted mood. When he came home from work, Lucky never left his side and I'd see him sneak him some table scraps when he thought no one was looking.

"One night when I was about twelve, Lucky howled and howled till dawn. I don't think I got any sleep at all. No matter what we tried, he wouldn't stop and we finally had to tie him up out back. When I left for the Old Bishop School that morning, so tired I could barely keep my eyes open, he was still wailing like a banshee. All these years later, I still get chills thinking about it. Later that morning, the principal of my school, a tall pale man who smelled like herring, pulled me out of class and said my father had died. Just like that. I don't know how I made it home crying my eyes out, but by the time I got there all the relatives had assembled and they were making arrangements, even with my father's body growing cold in the bedroom upstairs.

"Dogs know.

"So much for the theory that hard work never killed anyone. With an assist from Ma's cooking.

"Things changed quickly after that and not in a good way. The first thing Ma did was give Lucky away to a rich family in Palmer Woods on the other side of town, a terrible thing to do to a boy who was still grieving from losing his father. Lucky was just another mouth to feed, making me wonder if I was next. I never saw him again, except in a dream. Until now.

"Then, Ma drilled into my head that we were one step away from being out on the street and it was up to me as 'man of the house' to bring home money, so we wouldn't starve to death. She called me 'My *oreman* Meyer," which meant 'my poor Meyer.' Years later, when I learned about self-esteem on one of those TV talk shows, it explained a lot.

"After school, I got a paper route, selling the News on the corner of Fort and Shelby in the business district. My instructions, delivered with a stern broken-English warning, were not to come home until I sold every last one. What a thing to put on the shoulders of a kid. So I stood there like a schmuck in the bitter cold or the sweltering heat, sometimes past midnight, because I was afraid to walk in the door without all the money, which Ma had figured to the penny. What she lacked in verbal skills, she more than made up for in arithmetic.

"Once a week or so, Uncle Norman passed by my corner after coming out of Ziggy Fink's, a blind pig and gambling joint where all the big dice games were held. Win or lose, Uncle Norman always looked like a million bucks in his charcoal pin-stripe suit with a red boutonniere and black-and-white patent-leather wing-tips shined to such a high gloss you could see your own mug in the reflection. He'd reach in his pocket and tuck a couple of dollars in my hand, a lot of money in those days when the paper sold for two cents. Then he'd pick up my remaining bundle and drop it in the nearest trash can. "Go home, *shmendrik*. Give the money to your *balebusta* and keep a nickel for yourself," he'd say, favoring me with a wink, a tip of his pearl-gray fedora, and a jaunty wave as he continued on his way, those shoes clicking down the street.

"Uncle Norman was the greatest guy I knew, the closest thing I had to a role model, which is why I took it particularly hard when he blew his brains out a couple years later after losing his dry-cleaning business, his family, and everything else when the dice turned cold. Even at a young age, death seemed to follow me around like a puppy.

"It was a shame, especially in my father's case.

Had he lived, he most likely would have become a rich man like all the other junk dealers who sold their scrap to become 'industrialists' in the years leading up to World War II. And I would have been the son of a rich man with a sizable inheritance, instead of just another *zjlub* struggling to make something of myself.

"Because I was small for my age and wore wire-rimmed glasses with Coke-bottle lenses, bullies routinely tried to beat me up and take my money. But I was more afraid of Ma than I was of them, so I fought back like a lunatic, pummeling them with wild punches that found their mark more often than not. It was a good education; sometimes you gotta get slapped around to find out what you're made of. Remember that. It could come in handy. Once you get punched in the nose, you figure out it doesn't hurt as bad as you thought. Soon I learned about keeping a roll of nickels hidden away in my hand, a poor-boy's brass knuckles. After I knocked out enough teeth to make a whole new set, word got around and the bigger kids left me alone to find easier prey.

"And because I kept falling asleep in class, I got kicked out of the eighth grade. Luckily, I graduated from peddling papers to washing sheets at Superior Linen Supply, a job on a par with shoveling manure out of the world's biggest stable. That's where I learned what pigs people can be, all the disgusting stains and spots that turned my stomach inside out. But it paid better and it was indoors, so I thought it was a step up.

"It was me and my pals Sammy Rappaport,

Joey Herman, Hymie Mitnick, Irv Factor, and Jack Shorr, guys from the neighborhood who came up more or less the same way I did. We worked hard, never complained, and kept our heads down, but always aspired to a better situation. It must have worked, because we came to the attention of the owner's son, Abner Greenbaum, a mean little bastard with a chip on his shoulder and a mouth that always pointed toward the floor. He liked us, though, because soon he kicked us upstairs to the delivery department, where we got to drive a Ford truck that was beat all to hell, but looked like a Cadillac to us.

"Sammy Rappaport and I were teamed up together. I was older, which meant I got to drive, and he made the laundry deliveries, mainly because he was a big muscular kid, a *shtarker* who never got tired. With his pale skin and head full of wavy red hair, he looked more Irish than Jewish, which kept the other kids from picking on us or stealing our money. Plus, I still had my reputation as a tough little *pisher* who could dish it out and take it. Fortunately, Sammy took care of most of the dirty work. One time, some Litvak son-of-a-bitch tried to pull a fast one, but Sammy put him down fast with one punch to his midsection that made a sound like a tire exploding."

Meyer stopped, looked up at the ceiling, and pulled twice on his right earlobe, as if it would trigger a memory. At last he said, "This would have been around 1924, which made me fifteen. It was a full six years after Prohibition passed in Michigan—we were the first state in the country to go for that harebrained scheme; I could have told them you can't get people to quit drinking by passing a law, but nobody asked me. After a couple months of proving ourselves, Greenie would give us some after-hours jobs that involved going down to the Detroit River and picking up crates of whiskey imported on little boats from Windsor on the Canadian side. The 'Little Jewish Navy,' the papers called them, and there were way too many to stop, bringing in enough booze to raise the river a couple of feet at least. Every now and then the cops paid us a visit, but Greenie always gave us a few bucks to schmear them and make them look the other way.

"We didn't know it then, but we were working for what would become the Purple Gang, Detroit's Jewish version of the Mafia. Rumor has it they got their name because a couple of old shopkeepers on Chene Street said they were rotten as purple, the color of bad meat. But inside the gang, they just called themselves 'the Boys.'

"Jewish kids had a reputation for being sissies; you could steal their lunches and break their violins. But not these Jews. They were the toughest bastards you'd ever want to meet. Wouldn't take crap from nobody. And they were ambitious, moving up the ladder from muggings and petty theft to hijacking, extortion, prostitution, and eventually murder. A lot of murder. The blood ran freely, I can tell you that.

"But not me. One thing I got from Ma was a good head for numbers. I could do my multiplication tables and percentages at lightning speed without writing them down. So Greenie gave me my own route, collecting proceeds from dice games and bookmaking operations run by the Boys. I never came up short, not even once, and he rewarded me with two percent off the top, which amounted to an extra twenty or thirty bucks a week, a king's ransom to a kid like me, more than enough to get Ma squared away and still dress sharp and take a girl out from time to time. In a strange way, it felt like payback for Uncle Norman. The dice may have killed him, but they were saving me."

Meyer finally paused to take a breath. Or maybe it was a sigh. You know how people say, "I'm fading fast?" Well, that was Meyer, but not just figuratively. I saw him growing fainter by the second; when I looked at him, I could actually make out the country-patterned wallpaper.

"My memory's shot. We'll finish up another time." He paused for a moment and cocked his head, as though listening to something far way. At length he said, "There's a guy here says he knows you. Big fella, bald, looks like one of those wrestlers on TV. He's got a message for you. Hang tough. That's it. He's gone." It was the last thing Meyer said before dissolving out of view, as if someone had turned his dimmer switch all the way down.

I had a million more questions. Like what was he doing here? And why? But I knew they would have to wait. One thing that couldn't wait was a bathroom run. My bladder, pressed in by the baby, desperately needed relieving.

When I got back, I rewound the tape recorder. It was a good thing I didn't completely trust the device to record a ghost and had scribbled notes furiously throughout Meyer's monologue, because at the end of the interview, the only thing I could hear was white noise sprinkled with a wah-wah sound that came and went at irregular intervals and gave me shivers up and down my spine. My guess was that this particular model wasn't designed to pick up audio from the Great Beyond. Someday, if I have time, I'll call their consumer hotline and lodge a complaint.

PART THREE

January—April

CHAPTER 36

"Do you want to know?" The ultrasound technician pointed to the screen. He was a slight Asian man who carried himself with an air of dignity. While he seemed certain, the image before us provided zero help to the untrained eye.

Aaron and I had both discussed it ahead of time and agreed it was a no-brainer. "Absolutely," he said. We were eager to get started on the nursery, among other things. And I was eager to win my bet.

"It's a boy."

Aaron took my hand in his and flashed a million-watt smile, the biggest I'd seen on his usually Zen-like kisser.

"And from the looks of him," the tech continued, "he's going to be quite a swordsman."

Aaron and the tech high-fived. So much for dignity. Still, I knew this was Aaron's moment. Once I learned our baby had all its fingers and toes and other essentials, I became less invested in its gender. I'd heard mothers-to-be express this same sense of relief many times in the past, and now I was following that well-traveled pathway. I guess the old clichés catch on for a reason.

Upon hearing this second bit of news, Aaron's smile grew even wider, something I didn't think possible.

"I made that," he said.

Now all that remained was for me to figure out how to get my hands on that hundy.

CHAPTER 37

Here's something you might not know. Bass players are really strong. You would be too if you spent three to four hours a night wielding a 15-pound block of wood, even with a strap. Not to mention lugging around a big old amp. Before leaving the Dickweeds, Aaron and the drummer had been their de facto roadies to save money, so he wound up doing a lot of the setup and teardown himself. That was why I wasn't surprised to see him traipsing across the kitchen with a bag of concrete under each arm. What did shock me was why he was schlepping concrete around in the first place. (But I wasn't surprised that I was starting to think in Yiddish.)

"Where do we keep the wheelbarrow around here?" he asked, like it was the most normal question in the world.

"Around here? As in the house we live in?"

"Yeah," he said, missing my point.

I let it go. "Have you tried the garage?"

"First place I looked."

"Did you move stuff around?"

"Sort of. I can tell it's not there."

"I suggest you check again." I moved forward in my chair like I was planning to stand, not the easiest trick these days. "Because if I have to go out there and find it myself, you're in big trouble." I shot him a look I'd appropriated from Mrs. Lundberg, my fifth-grade teacher.

He trudged back to the garage and a few minutes later he yelled, "Got it!" Followed by the squeak of wheels creaking under 120 pounds.

Later that afternoon, I had my answer. It came in a quartet of police sirens caterwauling in unison, if not harmony, growing closer by the second. Peering out the kitchen window, I satisfied my curiosity when a contingent of three Metro squad cars and a motorcycle squealed to a halt in front of the house, their migraine-inducing lights flashing haphazardly, four uniformed occupants exiting with purpose. As they approached and surrounded Aaron, hands hovering around their holsters, I cracked the window to get in clearer earshot of the conversation about to take place. If things went south in a hurry, I would still have time to waddle outside to assume the role of peacemaker. Although I knew Aaron wouldn't want me in harm's way, I also realized that seriously pregnant women posed little risk in the eyes of the law. And beneath it all, the reporter's thought, "Must be a slow news day."

"Sir, please put the shovel down and let me see your hands," the largest of the officers said with the authoritative politeness they must teach at the Academy. All the while delivering a clear message by patting his holster in a steady drumbeat with his right hand.

Aaron did as he was told, gently laying the shovel next to a rounded concrete ridge that ran the entire width of our street. I couldn't help smiling as I thought, that's my industrious boy.

"What seems to be the trouble, officer?" he asked.

"Do you have a permit for that, that, whatever it is you're building?" the big cop asked.

"Just a speed bump," Aaron said. "And no, I don't have a permit. Just the moral high ground. You have no idea how fast these construction vehicles come barreling through here all hours of the day and night. Sounds like a buffalo stampede every time. Not to mention all our ex-neighbors' moving vans. We're going to have a baby and I want to make sure he's born into a safe and quiet environment."

The cop rubbed his salt-and-pepper buzz cut with the palm of his hand before saying, "Have you considered moving?"

"No, sir. We love it here."

"Well, it's all very admirable. But unfortunately, against the law. We're going to need you to remove that bump immediately, before it sets and you have to rent a jackhammer."

"Yes, sir."

The cop looked at his comrades to make sure they were appeased. They all nodded, bobbleheads in blue.

"Do you mind if I ask a question?"

"Go ahead."

"Do you know who reported us?"

"Anonymous tip."

"Interesting, especially considering we're the only ones left. Other than Mr. Caldwell. And he's not going anywhere, either."

"A word of advice. Next time, please submit the proper paperwork before taking matters into your own hands."

"Will do. Have a nice day."

"You too."

As they headed out to harass the next scofflaw, Aaron wandered back to the kitchen, his face sweat-streaked and red.

"Nicely played," I said, laying a kiss on the one clean spot on his cheek.

"I was plenty nervous, believe me. But at least I learned a few things. We're being closely watched, for one."

"And the other?"

"Someone's got these cops in a hip pocket. They don't send out four vehicles for a bank robbery, let alone a little unauthorized construction." He paused to open the fridge and pop open a can of beer as a sly grin played across his lips. "Of course, I've got another trick up my sleeve. Want to know what it is?"

I shook my head. "When the time comes, surprise me."

❧O☙

Two days later, Aaron walked in with a heavy-duty knapsack slung over his shoulder. Lucky meandered over and gave the bag an obligatory sniff before returning to his sentry position at the side door.

"Watcha got there, Santa?"

The bag clattered and clunked as he dropped it at my feet.

"See for yourself," he said, his face barely containing a shit-eating grin.

The collection of body parts prompted a "Holy crap!" on my part as I reflexively jumped back in my chair.

"Plastic, of course," he continued. "From the Mannequin Store on DI. They're running a BOGO."

I laid my best fake-angry look on him. "You could have given me fair warning. I am with child, after all."

"What fun would that be? Besides, you said surprise you."

"Figure of speech."

He gave me a quick kiss, hoisted the sack, and headed for the door. "I'm off to spread the wealth."

"I don't even wanna know what that means."

That night, as we lay in bed under a canopy of preemptive mosquito netting, we heard the first of many big rigs slamming their air brakes in a misguided attempt to avoid the arms, legs, and heads strewn throughout the neighborhood. Proving that two, indeed, could play this game.

CHAPTER 38

"How about Peter?"

Aaron put down the copy of the book he was reading, something about life in feudal Japan. "Peter?"

"For the baby. After my father."

"Not this again," he said, sitting up on the couch to better deliver a disapproving look.

"I thought you'd be excited about this. We're running out of time." I knew he liked to let things percolate, but I needed to jumpstart the process.

"We've got plenty of time. Besides, no dick names."

I deflected his look and returned one of my own. "What do you mean?"

"Peter's a dick name. Literally. Like Lance, Willy, Rod, Woody. And, of course, Dick."

"That's funny coming from a guy who played in a band called 'the Dickweeds.'"

"A band's a band. This is different. You wouldn't name a kid Weezer either."

I considered it before circling back to the original subject. "So I guess we won't be naming the little fella Schlong."

Aaron chortled despite himself. "Where'd you learn a word like that?"

"Online. For an article I'm researching." Just the tiniest of white lies. Aaron seemed to buy it and I lunged ahead before he could ask a follow-up question. "Okay, what about Aaron, Jr.?"

He bit down on his lip and shook his head. "First of all, Jews don't name sons after their fathers. And second, I'd hate doing that to a kid. It's like trying to make him a little carbon copy of myself, before he can even develop his own identity. And it just causes confusion. You'll be yelling 'Aaron!' all the time when one of us is in trouble and we won't know which one should hide."

"Both, if you know what's good for you. Okay, smart guy. Your turn."

"No, it's not. I wasn't ready to play this game in the first place."

"Come on, be a good sport," I said. "Just one name. Then we can table this for a future discussion." Like tomorrow.

He stroked his chin and thought for what seemed like a long time. "How about Michael? Shortens to Mike, which has a strong sound to it. Timeless, you know? Not trendy. Biblical I'm pretty sure, an angel, in case we need to sell your folks on it. Mike Eisenberg. A nice flow, don't you think?"

Actually, I did think. It was the first time we'd thought to couple the first and last names, and it seemed to work. "You might be on to something there," I said. "But I don't want to settle, not just yet. I want to mull it over for a while."

"Mull all you want," Aaron said, clearly losing interest in the subject.

When he returned to his book, I looked up the name. It was of Hebrew origin, meaning "Gift from God." I took the goosebumps on my arms as a sign I could live with that.

CHAPTER 39

"So," I began, not exactly sure how to phrase my question. I drew in a breath and plowed ahead before I could wuss out. "What's it like? Being dead and all." We had so many balls in the air, I'd never thought to delve into the metaphysical implications until now.

Meyer raised an eyebrow. At that instant, I realized he was no longer translucent; whatever had been going on with his molecules or atoms had settled down and he appeared almost solid. And easily 20 years younger than the day he arrived in our guestroom unannounced. Not handsome by any means. But kind of dashing.

"I have no idea," he said.

His answer caught me off guard and my brain fumbled for a follow-up. "But, but ..." I had read all those obits. "You are dead, right?"

He tossed a slight sardonic smile my way. The seconds trickled by. Outside a gust of wind sent a tree branch into the side of the house with a loud smack and I gave a little jump in my chair. "That's the rumor," he said. "But to tell you the truth, I'm not the best person to ask. One minute I was nowhere. And now I'm here. Go figure."

"How do you account for that?"

"I can't. It doesn't make sense, any more than living makes sense."

"No heaven?"

"God no." He snorted at his own joke.

"No white light?"

He shook his head. "Dark as the bottom of a coal mine. At midnight."

"No departed relatives greeting you with open arms?"

"Not a one. Never liked them anyway." Then softly, "Except for my Ruthie. I miss her every day."

I felt a deep hole in the place my stomach usually occupied as I began to despair ever walking this path. My logical side always told me the afterlife was a comforting story made up by people who were afraid to die, which is pretty much all of us. Eternal oblivion, like Aaron says, just isn't that encouraging of a concept. But my emotional side had always held out hope. The whole "energy can neither be created nor destroyed" law had to count for something. No matter. Too late to turn back. Sometimes being a journalist really stinks.

"But," I continued, "no hell either?" Looking for a bright side.

"A good thing, too. Because I'm not sure all my charity work would've been, you know, enough."

I let it all sink in. "Well, you're no help at all."

He held up his palms in apology. "I can't say

I'm surprised. In the old days, I thought God was just another name for luck. People prayed to God. Sometimes it worked out, sometimes it didn't. If it did, they said God answered their prayers. If not, well, who were you to understand the plans of the Almighty? *Bubbe meises*, if you ask me. Old wives' tales. Horseshit plain and simple. You should pardon the expression."

"I've heard it," I said.

"When it comes right down to it, what's the difference between God and Santa Claus? Both old men with long white beards. And they know when you're sleeping and when you're awake. Kind of disturbing when you stop to think about it." Meyer shrugged.

"My God, you sound like my husband." I pushed onward. "Well, if that's the case, I guess there's no use asking you about the meaning of life."

"You'd be better off going to a rabbi or a priest or some other holy man," he said. "They seem to have all the answers. I sure as hell don't. Just 'cause you're dead doesn't make you all-knowing. Or even smart."

My face reddened in frustration, my one chance at understanding the infinite slipping away.

"But I can tell you this."

I leaned forward, maybe in response to the slightest inkling of faith.

"I think I figured it out when I was still alive. At least in a way I could understand."

"I'm all ears."

"It's that little kids' song. Row your boat."

I sat all the way back and sunk into the cushion, defeated.

"You're kidding."

"Never kid a kidder. How's it start?"

"Row, row, row your boat," I offered.

"Right. Notice it says 'row your boat.' Not someone else's. You gotta be responsible for yourself, make your own way in this world. Your world."

Meyer was drawing me in despite myself. Maybe this wasn't a complete waste of time after all.

"If I remember correctly, and who knows these days, it says, 'gently down the stream.'"

"Uh-huh."

"So you don't row hard, you row easy. And you don't fight the current; you go with the flow, as the hippies used to say."

Not bad. I could envision collaborating with Meyer on a children's book.

He sang the next verse in a croaky off-key voice. "'Merrily, merrily, merrily, merrily.' You're here. You didn't ask to be here, but here you are. So you might as well make the best of it."

I had to admit he had a point.

"Sing the last verse with me. It's my favorite," Meyer said.

Together we sort of harmonized, "Life is but a dreeeeeem," finishing with a ragged flourish before dissolving into laughter. The White Stripes we weren't.

"It is, you know. A dream," he said finally. "Or a nightmare." His expression going from pleased to gloomy in a heartbeat. "It's up to us."

"That's really profound," I said, reaching to pat his hand. Instinctively, he pulled away.

"I don't think that's such a good idea."

"Why not?"

He shook his head slowly. "No reason. I just don't."

I didn't want our conversation to end on such a down note, so I joked, "You're a real buzzkill."

"I don't know what that means, but I think I can figure it out. We Jews are like that. Behind every cloud there's a silver lining. But you know what's behind that?"

"Another cloud?"

"Smart girl. I think it's the reason we survived all these years. Hope for the best, but expect the worst."

I could relate to that, especially lately. But it didn't mean I had to like it. "It sure sucks the fun out of life."

"Or death."

At that moment, I didn't feel like such a smart girl. Having a philosophical discussion with a ghost. Who still might be a figment of my pregnant imagination.

As if seeing right through me, Meyer asked, "When all is said and done, what the hell difference does it make?"

A question I couldn't answer at the moment.

CHAPTER 40

"What's wrong?" I asked, clicking the Zumba Fitness infomercial to mute. I couldn't do the exercises any more, but I could sure as hell watch them and eat my heart out.

Aaron closed the front door, shrugged his shoulders, and gave me back a blank stare. "Nothing."

I knew from the black cloud hovering over his head that his response wasn't entirely accurate. But I also knew better than to press him on it. At least, not too much.

"Okay, if you feel like talking, you know where to find me." Right here on this couch logging quality TV time in between bouts of insomnia and feeling sorry for myself.

He trudged to the kitchen where I saw the reflected light of the refrigerator and heard the popping of a can. A moment later, he reappeared in the living room with a Coors light and the basset-hound expression.

"Work was pretty shitty tonight," he offered finally, taking a gulp and falling into the recliner.

I returned his gaze with what I hoped was a supportive one of my own. And waited. And waited.

Then, “It’s that douchebag Schroeder. He handed me a new playlist right before the show and said we need to learn the songs by Friday. Eighties’ sadboy shit, the worst crap imaginable. ABC. Howard Jones. Naked Eyes. Flock of Fucking Seagulls. The guy’s what, twenty-five? Twenty-six? What makes him think he knows how to run a lounge?”

“His father owns the casino?”

Aaron forced a smile, but it didn’t take. “Besides that.”

“Well, what are your options?”

He stared intently at his beer. “I could quit, I guess.”

“Okay.” I exhaled sharply and tried to keep my expression from revealing that quitting was a really bad idea at the moment.

“Or I could suck it up and do what he says.”

Better. “I know you don’t have a lot of experience working for other people, but this kind of thing happens all the time,” I said. “When you’re an employee, a certain amount of eating shit just naturally comes with the job.”

“Doesn’t seem fair. But I understand what you’re saying.”

“Or ...”

“Yeah?”

“You could push back. Make him see the error of his ways.”

He shook his head. “It’ll never work. That little

prick thinks he knows everything. Besides, I'm not that persuasive."

"I don't know about that. Less than a day after I met you, you got me to move across the country to a city I'd only seen on the Travel Channel."

"The Eisenberg charm doesn't work on dudes." He paused for a moment. "Too bad life isn't like 'The Sopranos.' Whenever Tony ran into a roadblock, he'd just break someone's kneecap. Or whack him. That's mobster talk, you know."

I knew. "It would make things simpler."

"But the real world doesn't work that way," he said forlornly. Downing the last of his beer, he gave me a peck on the lips and said, "I'll sleep on it. Maybe I'll wake up with a bright idea."

"Instead of just a boner?"

He smiled for real this time. "I love it when you talk dirty. Don't stay up too late."

I heard him tromping up the stairs. Not too late, I thought. But first I needed to work on a bright idea of my own.

Next night, same time, same couch, same husband. Different attitude. A complete 180, as a matter of fact. Aaron nearly danced in, not an easy task for a man with two left feet. I felt like dancing myself, the sense of relief and exhilaration profound.

"What's gotten into you?" I asked, having a fairly good idea already.

"Guess," he said, rocking back and forth like a little boy with a full bladder.

I'm not a big fan of guessing, but figured I'd make an exception. Might even be fun.

"You hit Megabucks?"

He shook his head. "You set the bar pretty high."

"Okay, I'll go lower. They comped your dinner tonight." I was getting good at talking that Vegas lingo.

Aaron feigned disappointment. "Not that low."

"I give up."

"Schroeder had a change of heart. Or what passes for a heart. He came up to me right before our first set, all nervous and shit, and said not to worry about the new song list. He did some asking around and found out the eighties' crowd doesn't spend a lot of money on booze." Aaron waltzed over to the couch and deposited a big kiss on my lips. He smelled like second-hand smoke and stale beer, the signature fragrance of his chosen profession. "He even said I could mix in an original song from time to time."

"That's great!" I said, returning his affection. "I'm so happy for you. For us."

"Things have a way of working out sometimes, I suppose. That's a new concept for me."

"Get used to it, mister. This is just the beginning. We're on a roll."

"I like the sound of that. Think I'll take a quick shower. Meet me upstairs in fifteen?"

Code for let's have congratulatory sex. And why not? If he could stand my Jabba the Hut body, I was sure it would do us both some good.

He started up the stairs, stopped halfway, scratched his head and muttered, “I wish I knew what got into that guy.”

“You stop that right now,” I said in my best school principal’s voice. “Don’t you look this gift horse in the mouth.”

“I guess you’re right,” he said before disappearing into the second floor hallway. I heard the bathroom door click shut, followed by creaking pipes indicating the shower in progress.

I knew what got into the guy. But I’d never tell.

The phone call had gone like this. “Mr. Schroeder, this is Anna Eisenberg, Aaron’s wife.” My heart raced like a Corvette. I took a deep breath and down-shifted into third.

“Who?” he squealed, sounding no more than ten. A real *pisher*. Vegas lingo wasn’t the only kind I’d been picking up lately.

“Aaron. Your bass player.”

“Right. For the house band. What can I do for you, Mrs. Essleman?”

“Eisenberg. It’s about the new playlist. Aaron hates it. He won’t play those songs.”

A pause. “You do realize I could go downstairs, throw a rock, and hit a dozen bass players just dying for a steady gig.”

“But you won’t.”

An amused snicker. “You’ve got balls, I’ll give you that. Enlighten me. Why won’t I?”

“Mr. Schroeder, are you familiar with the Israeli mob?”

Longer pause. “Not personally, no.”

"And you'd like to keep it that way, I assume?"

His voice went up half an octave, something I didn't think possible. "What are you getting at exactly?"

"Wellll," I stretched the word out, savoring the suspense. "Just a quick genealogy lesson. Are you familiar with the name Max Eisenberg?"

"Can't say that I am."

"Max was Aaron's grandfather. They called him 'Ice Pick.' Want to know why?"

"Not especially."

"It's just as well. You could google him if you're really interested. Something to do with labor relations in Chicago during the Depression."

"Look, I've got a lounge to run. So if you're done with the obscure history lesson ..."

"Not quite. Max immigrated to Israel in the early sixties where, fairly late in life, he begat a son." Nice. A biblical reference. I was quite enjoying this. "Ari Eisenberg, who made a name for himself as a, shall we say, eraser. Not the kind found in school. And then, in 1985, Ari begat a son of his own. My very own Aaron. Who's still very close to his father, in case you were wondering."

"I wasn't."

"You should be. So a word of advice. Throw away the fucking playlist. And if you breathe a word of this to the bass player, his father is going to pay you a visit very late at night. When you least expect it. *Farshteyn*?"

"I beg your pardon?"

"You dig?"

I swear I could hear him gulp as he choked out

a meek, "Yes, ma'am."

I hung up before he could say anything else, pumping my fist in triumph. Only then did I realize I'd been pacing the room like a prisoner in solitary. To cover my tracks, I brushed my foot over the path I'd worn in the carpet. No reason to leave any evidence. Now all I needed was to wait patiently for my husband to come home and deliver the good news. In about seven hours. Easier said than done. While I was ninety-nine percent sure Schroeder would knuckle under, that small nagging voice began buzzing around my brain like a gnat. "What if he says something? What if he fires Aaron? What if, what if, what if?"

To shut it up, I made a trip to the fridge and extracted the remainder of the authentic Detroit-style chili I'd badgered Aaron into picking up from Motor City Hot Dogs (late one night to quell a screaming pregnancy fit), along with an ice-cold Vernor's, only the best ginger ale on the planet. Just what the doctor didn't order. Screw her; she didn't have my cravings. After heating it up in the microwave (the only "cooking" I could manage these days), I settled back onto the couch to wolf down my self-congratulatory meal.

Concocting the backstory had been surprisingly easy. I just googled "Eisenberg" and "mobster" and there, toward the bottom of the first page, I found what I needed: Max Eisenberg, a connected Depression-era labor leader, Chicago-style. The "Ice Pick" nickname and Israeli mob father I made up to add a sense of danger and authenticity. The best lies, I was learning, always started with a kernel of truth. If Schroeder even bothered to fact-check my tall tale, which I doubted, the Internet would provide just enough confirmation.

No more getting pushed around by little shit-heads in positions of authority. I had a house and a family to protect.

I rather liked the new me.

CHAPTER 41

"Listen to your horoscope," Aaron said over Sunday breakfast. "'The only way out is through.'"

I had no idea what that meant. But it didn't matter. To my mind, looking at your spouse's horoscope is yet another sign of true love. But I was too preoccupied at the moment. "I'm worried," I said. "I haven't seen Mr. Caldwell in a while. The papers are piling up and the trash can's been out on the curb since Wednesday. That's not like him."

Aaron took a last swig of coffee, made a face, and said, "Have you gone over there? Tried knocking?"

"No. He'd probably just come to the door and think I was being silly." I tried to keep my hands from fluttering around like hummingbirds, which sometimes happens when I'm all *verklempt*.

"Well, let's check it out," he said, placing the mug on top of his plate and pushing both away from the edge of the table. "No time like the present."

"You sound like my dad. He's got a million of those old sayings."

"They say girls marry their fathers. And boys marry their mothers."

"Ick."

We looked both ways before crossing the street, a habit we'd developed to avoid getting flattened by one of the many dump trucks or skip loaders making the rounds all hours of the day or night. Arriving on the other side in one piece, we spent the next fifteen minutes knocking, ringing the doorbell, and trying to peer through the windows into the darkened house, a task made more difficult by the drawn blinds.

"I have a bad feeling about this," I said, and the baby seemed to kick in agreement. "Think we should call nine-one-one? What if it turns out to be nothing?"

"They take you to jail. But it's okay. I'll bail you out when I get paid."

"Comforting. I think it's better to be safe than sorry." I stopped and tilted my head. "Listen to me. Now I sound like my dad."

But Aaron hadn't heard; he was too busy punching the number into his phone.

"The nature of my emergency?" he repeated. "Well, I'm not sure it's an actual emergency. Not yet, anyway. We haven't seen our neighbor all week. He's old and we're worried about him." They prattled on for another minute, ending with Aaron giving the dispatcher Mr. Caldwell's address. "Yes, we'll stay. Thank you."

Less than a half-hour later, quick by Vegas standards, but 20 minutes longer than it took for the cops to shut down Aaron's little speed-bump escapade, a Metro car pulled up in front of Mr. Caldwell's house, driven by the big officer I recognized from his previous appearance, apparently assigned to our neighborhood for life or until we moved, whichever came first.

"You the folks who called this in?"

Aaron raised his hand like a basketball player acknowledging a foul. "It was me, officer."

"Seen any plastic body parts lately?" the cop asked.

If the question caught Aaron off guard, he didn't let on. "No, sir."

But the cop had already moved on to the business at hand. Briefly surveilling the situation, he asked, "What prompted your concern?"

I said, "See all those newspapers in the driveway? Mr. Caldwell never misses a day. He's very meticulous. So we knocked on his door this morning. No answer. Walked all around the house, peered in the windows. It's quiet as can be in there." Deathly quiet, I thought, despite myself.

He wrote something in his notepad before asking, "Could he be out of town? Any relatives you know of?"

"None. But even if he did, I'm sure he'd put the paper on hold before leaving."

"How well do you know him?"

"Not that well, but we talked all the time. He's our favorite neighbor."

"What's his approximate age?"

"Late sixties, early seventies maybe. He served in Vietnam."

"Health conditions of any kind?"

I remembered back to the meeting and the reality of the situation came crashing down on me. “He said he had bad hips. And a bum ticker.” I could barely get the words out.

Officer McMahon, according to his name tag, strode to Mr. Caldwell’s Semper Fidelis mailbox, opened the little door, and pulled out a big pile of papers, everything from the Wednesday store flyers to envelopes of every size and color. Sorting through each piece, he said, “Looks like he hasn’t been around since early in the week.” Unclipping a black LED flashlight from his utility belt, he took his time doing a 360 of the house, while we stood on the driveway holding hands and trying to stay out of the way.

“No sign of forced entry,” he said after inspecting the perimeter. “Think we’d better call in a locksmith.” He went back to the patrol car and fiddled with some equipment before making his call.

We sat on the curb, trying to think of logical explanations other than the worst one, but came up short. At last, a tired old van featuring a hand-lettered Hometown Lock and Key sign and faded key clipart groaned to a stop in front. The driver, a roly-poly middle-aged man with “Duck Dynasty” whiskers, set the brake with a yank, exited the vehicle, rusted green toolbox in hand, and greeted Officer McMahon with obligatory small talk before hobbling toward the house. Literally 20 seconds later, the front door popped open. The locksmith made it look so easy that I wondered how quickly someone who knew what they were doing could break into our house. Officer McMahon scribbled his name on the service-call invoice, handing it to the man before cautiously entering Mr. Caldwell's.

When the big cop emerged a short time later, the grim look on his face told me all I needed to know.

"Sorry, folks. Afraid I've got bad news. Looks like he passed in his sleep. Can I ask one of you some questions? For my report? It won't take long." Almost compassionate. I wondered what Pykowski would have to say about that.

"I'll do it," Aaron volunteered.

After all the emotional turmoil of the preceding months, I couldn't believe I had more tears to shed. But they seemed to be in endless supply. For Mr. Caldwell, of course. But for us as well. Sitting there on the curb, staring into space, I had never felt so utterly, hopelessly, alone.

~O~

That evening, I said to Lucky, "I wish you could talk. I need someone to tell me everything's going to be okay."

From the laundry room, where Boozer was folding socks and shouting, "Ding! Ding! Ding!" every time he got a match, he yelled, "Everything's going to be okay!" I swear the man has the hearing of a bat.

"I mean someone believable."

CHAPTER 42

The pressure and bad news must have gotten to me, because the contractions started in earnest later that week. At first, I assumed they were Braxton Hicks, early random contractions I'd learned about in health class, but they soon progressed, if you could call it that, to the painful kind that built in intensity at regular intervals. A fevered spin around the Web convinced me that a trip to the OB/GYN was in order, seeing as how I was only in week 29, give or take, out of a normal 40.

"You have an incompetent cervix," Dr. Kasden said after a thorough pelvic exam. She was a slight redheaded woman, not much older than me, with a child's voice that gave me pause the first time I met her, until I remembered my father's advice about medical professionals: Hire a young doctor and an old lawyer. And she (unlike my cervix) certainly seemed competent enough, although a bit reserved, possibly compensating for her girlish appearance.

Hearing the diagnosis, Aaron and I exchanged a look, each knowing what the other was thinking:

Incompetent Cervix would be a good name for a band. But this was no time for jokes. In fact, with the prospect of a preemie in the offing, I could feel myself developing a severe case of hives.

"What does that mean, exactly?" I asked in a cracked voice, while Aaron sat there stoically with a shell-shocked expression I remembered from finals week at college. I hoped he wasn't thinking that all this medical stuff was more than he'd signed up for.

The doctor continued, "Normally, a woman's cervix should open with the beginning of labor after about nine months of pregnancy. But in some women, for reasons unknown, pressure from the developing fetus causes the cervix to open early. That's what's happening in your case. Unfortunately, it can lead to premature birth or even spontaneous loss of pregnancy."

I felt the tears begin to well up. "You mean a miscarriage?"

"Actually, it's called stillbirth at this stage. But I'm afraid so."

As I attempted to process this news, Aaron stepped into the breach. "Surely there must be some form of treatment."

"We have a few options at our disposal," Dr. Kasden said. "The recommended course of action is weekly progesterone supplementation. While that can help and I recommend it, your best bet is to limit activity as much as possible. That means staying at home, no unnecessary movement, and conceivably even complete bedrest if the contractions don't subside or continue to get worse."

Again, my mind giggled inappropriately at the word "conceivably," no doubt a defense mechanism putting up a massive firewall against the bad news.

"Of course, if these actions prove ineffective, we may need to consider a transvaginal cerclage ..." I zoned out for a few seconds as I considered her use of the phrase "of course" in this context, as if I were one of her medical residents instead of just another scared patient. Fortunately, I picked up the conversational thread just in time to hear her say, "... but because of the invasive nature of the procedure, let's consider it a last resort." Which I was only too happy to do.

After answering a couple more questions, Dr. Kasden insisted I take a wheelchair down to our car, not only making me feel more vulnerable than ever, but drawing sidelong pity glances from each person we passed. I already suffered from varicose veins, hemorrhoids, constipation, and a host of other revolting maladies. And now this.

When I finally took a break from feeling sorry for myself, I reflected on the irony of it all. As quickly as my world had expanded, that's how fast it was contracting, no puns intended. For the foreseeable future, I would be housebound, if not downright bedridden.

Thank goodness I loved my house.

CHAPTER 43

As long as I was stuck in the house anyway, I welcomed Meyer's mid-afternoon appearance. With no preliminaries—no hello, how are ya', how's the dog—he told me he remembered enough to continue his life story. Or maybe that was what passed for preliminaries in his circles. I didn't bother with the tape recorder this time, and although my fingers were as fat as overstuffed sausages, they still worked well enough to chronicle his recollections.

"Like I said, I was good with numbers. Even though I had little formal schooling, arithmetic came easy to me. I could add a column of figures in my head without breaking a sweat. Same with percentages. So when Tommy Jordan got bumped off for skimming too much from his dice game, they gave me his action. A good lesson. You can get away with a lot if you don't get too greedy. A little off the top was expected; these were gangsters, after all. Everybody got their taste, just like the government. But the unwritten rule was, not so much you'd draw attention to yourself. That's how you wound up on the fast track to early retirement of the permanent kind. Plus, when you had a good thing going, you didn't want to fuck it up."

Meyer paused for a moment and I could see the crimson wash over his features. "No offense," he mumbled.

"None taken." It was the first time the old man had dropped an F-bomb in my presence and I could tell he was genuinely embarrassed.

"I hate it when I forget my manners in front of a lady."

For some reason, I liked that he referred to me as a lady. It seemed quaint and flattering at the same time.

He continued, "I was also good with people. I certainly knew when to keep my mouth shut, which I'd learned only too well from my father. But I also knew when to offer my opinion, how to compliment someone and make it sound sincere, when to give in, and when to get tough. That's not something you learn in school. You either have it or you don't. No matter, I always remembered my place. The last thing you wanted was a reputation for being too big for your britches. That's how you got a twenty-two slug in the back of the head, the one you never saw coming.

"One thing you could say about the Boys, they rewarded loyalty and initiative. In my case, it paid off in spades, because I ran an honest game. There was no reason to cheat with a big house edge in my favor and the players plunging on the field and hard ways and any seven, prop bets that cleaned them out as effectively as any pickpocket. And they all had the fever, so they couldn't stay away. Meanwhile, I'm comping them to top-shelf booze, the finest Havanas, and a little extra attention from the female shills who looked like poor-man's versions of Jean Harlow and Mae West."

I had no idea who Meyer was referring to, but I assumed they might be movie stars or supermodels back in the day. So I nodded and he went on with his story.

"And when they were down to their last nickel, we slipped them a buck, put them in a jitney, and sent them home. It was important to leave them with a few coins in their pockets and a shred of dignity. If you burn a guy, vacuum him like a Hoover, he's got a chip on his shoulder; he bad-mouths you all over town. Somehow it's your fault and that's bad for business. But you treat him like a mensch, a standup guy, he becomes a walking advertisement for your operation. That's why it never bothered me when somebody made a big score. You can't buy that kind of publicity—especially in a business that isn't exactly legal.

"So our numbers went through the roof month after month, year after year, along with my percentage. Before long, I was running every game Downriver. We schmeared the cops, the judges, the politicians, and they mostly left us alone. From time to time, they had to bust us for appearances, but they always warned us beforehand, which eased the pain. Bosses came and went, but I stuck around and made a nice living long after the Purple Gang fell apart from too much sloppiness and infighting. Even when the New York mob moved in and swept house, they kept me on, because they knew they could trust me. And I knew where the bodies were buried. Never underestimate the value of institutional knowledge.

"I could've gone on like that forever, but then the goddamn Japs bombed Pearl Harbor, caught us with our pants down, and everything changed. I was grateful for the opportunities our country had given me, so I was first in line at the enlistment office the next morning. I was almost thirty-two, old by military standards, but they were taking guys all the way up to forty-five. So in spite of my bad eyes and flat feet, the Army Air Corps issued me a uniform two sizes too big, boots two sizes too small, and a pair of GI horn-rimmed glasses and shipped me off for ten weeks to godforsaken Sheppard Field in Wichita Falls, Texas. They didn't have enough rifles in those days, so we trained with wooden ones, which didn't do us a helluva lot of good; we were more like kids playing bang-bang games, except for the drill sergeant who kept spitting in our faces and insulting our mothers.

"After basic, I wound up at Ellsworth Air Force Base in Rapid City, South Dakota. Because I could boil an egg, they assigned me to the mess hall, where I learned the essential skills of washing vegetables, peeling potatoes, and scraping dishes. That's where I discovered the power of steaks, chops, and chili con carne as currency. I could trade them with the brass for almost anything, which usually involved a leave of absence. I developed a reputation as a man who could get his hands on whatever someone wanted and before long, I parlayed that into a series of promotions that left me as a staff sergeant running my own mess hall.

"Every six months or so, they shipped me somewhere else, like a gun for hire on that Paladin TV show. I kept thinking I'd wind up on the front lines in Europe or the Pacific, but it never happened. I did get to see exotic locations like Boise, Idaho; Wendover, Utah (where I froze my *tuches* off); and Needles, California, the closest thing to hell on Earth. Hard to believe I spent three and a half years in the military during a world war and never left the country. The only action I ever saw was the weekly poker games, where I routinely cleaned out my bunk mates and tripled my ninety-six-dollars-a-month salary, most of which I shipped home to Ma. Nobody seemed to mind, because I always brought a bottle of first-class hooch to the game and I never stayed in one place long enough to wear out my welcome.

"Toward the end of 1944, I started training on a top-secret mission at Kirtland Army Air Field near Albuquerque, New Mexico, in glider planes so big they held tanks, jeeps, hundreds of troops, even a fully equipped mess hall, which is where I came in. Rumors were flying around like moths that we were going to be part of the invasion of Japan that would end the war once and for all. It would have likely been the end of me, too. But then Truman, God bless him, dropped the Bomb twice and that was that. I was lucky that way.

"Back in Detroit, I thought it would be business as usual. But it didn't take long to realize everything had changed. A whole new crop of cops, judges, and politicians had taken over from the old ones who'd been on our payroll, and they were young, mean, and looking to make a name for themselves. When they started cracking down on the games, it became almost impossible to make an honest living. I tried my hand at a couple new enterprises, like selling hot-water heaters door to door (that we acquired for pennies on the dollar because, well, let's just say they were a little warm), but nothing panned out.

"Well, almost nothing. Every Friday evening, I stopped by Sanders Ice Cream Parlor on Woodward for a hot fudge sundae. That's where I met Ruthie, the waitress who brought me my order every week. She was a hard-working gal and the prettiest thing I'd ever seen, like that actress, I can't think of her name, from that movie about the custody trial with the little Jewish actor with the big nose. My memory, though it seems to be returning, still hasn't been so good since I've been, you know, deceased. Anyway, I started walking her home after work; she lived with her brothers in a duplex near Gratiot, and before long they were giving me the third degree about my intentions toward their sister. I was already in love by then, so I asked her to marry me and she said yes and it was the best decision I ever made. She was a good girl who went along every time we moved, even though it was hard for her, and she stuck by me when I got sick, and she never complained. Not once.

"And that first move after we tied the knot was a doozy. Because it was becoming clear to me that Detroit was played out. I needed a fresh start, maybe someplace warmer like Florida. Not to mention friendly to my line of employment. I was lucky to be courted by some New York associates as a consultant for the new American gambling operations in Havana, mainly the Riviera and Nacional, to oversee the joints and make sure everyone was getting a fair shake, and to cozy up to Batista, the dictator, and keep him happy with regular payoffs. The humidity and bugs were ferocious, but it was a good gig, and the big bosses gave me a piece of the pie to boot. Ruthie and I could have stayed there indefinitely if it wasn't for Castro and the revolution, which had started up before we got there and really came to a head in 1959.

"Well, I always had a nose for trouble and staying out of the line of fire. But it didn't take much sniffing to know that Batista's days were numbered, along with all his associates, which included me. We were in serious hot water if we didn't get the hell out of Dodge. Couriers and bag ladies had been carrying out cash for weeks. Then, on a moonless night, we packed up our basic belongings and the rest of the money from the two cages and fled the island on a fishing boat to the sounds of gunshots ringing out in the distance, just a few days before the Generalissimo himself boarded a plane for the Dominican Republic, loaded down with his closest supporters and hundreds of millions in dollars and gold.

"No sooner had we crossed into international-al waters than a seaplane touched down. I'll tell you, climbing off that boat onto the plane in the dark was a hell of an experience even for me and I'd been in the Air Corps. For Ruthie, well, she talked about it for the rest of her life. The plane took us the rest of the way to Miami, where I handed over the remaining cash, every penny of it. The bosses gave us a few days of R & R at the Fontainebleau, then Ruthie and I caught a seven-oh-seven to Las Vegas, where they'd set me up with ownership points at the Capri Hotel-Casino, another ground-floor opportunity as part of the second wave of expansion that included the Dunes, Stardust, Riviera, and Tropicana. I thought the Gaming Control Board might give me a hard time, considering my past. But you know, I'd never been convicted or even charged with a serious crime and some new friends greased the skids with the right people. So I sailed through."

A knock on the door interrupted Meyer's narrative as a heavily accented Hispanic voice shouted, "Hello, missus! Are you there?"

"Sorry, Meyer. Be right back."

"No problem. I've got all the time in the world."

I opened the front door to find Julio, one of two workers we'd hired to replace the bannister on the exterior stairs leading to the second story.

"Can I have a glass of cold water? We ran out." Behind him, the sounds of a wimpy male singer escaped from his vintage 1980s boom box: "I'm all out of love ..."

"Of course, you poor man. Would you like one for your partner too?"

"Yes, ma'am. That would be nice."

As I prepared two glasses of ice water, the music changed to an even weaker lyric, "Have you never been mellow," making me briefly wonder about those burly construction workers before returning to Meyer and his story.

"They're putting the finishing touches on the railing," I told him. "One of the last projects before this place is officially fixer-upped." My statement was a revelation to me the moment I said it. "Wow. We're almost done."

Meyer smiled. "And every time you do something, I swear I feel more like my old self."

Before I could respond or even make sense of his words, he continued, "Now, where was I? Oh, yeah, anyway, I took to Vegas like a lame duck out of water. For the first time in my life, I didn't have to look over my shoulder all the time, worried that someone was trying to put me in jail or run me out of town or worse. It felt good to be a hundred percent legit. Since I could be anyone I wanted to be, I became a businessman. I wasn't a young man anymore, already in my mid-fifties, and I could finally give Ruthie the kind of life she deserved—a big bank account, no threat hanging over us from the authorities or taxman, and most of all, a husband who worked an eight-hour shift and was home for dinner. Maybe I felt guilty about all the things I put her through and wanted to make it up to her. Jews don't have the market cornered on guilt, but it is one of our specialties.

"We lived in the penthouse of the Capri for the first six months until we got our bearings straight. Then we bought a beautiful ranch house out in the suburbs in a neighborhood they called the Scotch Eighties, where our neighbors were casino owners, entertainers, real estate moguls, and other big *machers*. The only problem was once you got away from the Strip and the grind joints downtown, there wasn't much to Las Vegas in those days. No real shopping centers, high-class restaurants, not even a Reform temple. And God forbid you should develop a heart condition or even a hemorrhoid. People would say, 'Where's the first place you go if you get sick in Las Vegas?' And the answer was always 'McCarran.' You know, the airport. And they weren't joking. Even the governor headed for L.A. when he needed his gallbladder out.

"Well, that was unacceptable. It was the same old story, find a need and fill it. When I realized nobody else was going to take the bull by the horns, I put together my own crew, guys with dough, investors that read like a Who's Who of southern Nevada. And we started our own company, Eden Development. You ask, what did I know about the construction business? *Gornisht*, *bupkes*, nothing, that's what. But I knew plenty about project management and cash flow and for the rest of it, I surrounded myself with people who were smarter than me. And we made things happen, just like with bootlegging and the dice games.

"Within five years, we opened Sunset Hospital, the Parkway Mall, and the Desert Canyon Golf Club. And in ten years, I had my Reform synagogue, Temple Ner Simcha. Not that I was ever religious, but you get older, you start thinking about things. I figured it couldn't hurt. And when we were done, the only thing this town still needed was a good deli.

"I didn't realize it then, but I was building quite a legacy for myself and Ruthie. We could never have children, so maybe this was a way of leaving my mark. And people noticed. They began to hand out awards like they were going out of style. Chamber of Commerce Man of the Year, B'nai B'rith Torch of Liberty, Rotary's Distinguished Service, and a whole bunch more, enough to fill a wheelbarrow. Not bad for an old racketeer with an eighth-grade education.

"Naturally, we found ourselves doing a lot of entertaining. You can't very well ask folks for money and not feed them and ply them with drinks. That's when we realized the house was too small. So we built our own from the ground up, the very one you and your husband have adopted, which gives me so much *nachas* I can't tell you. You're in good company. Over the years, this place has seen everyone from Sinatra and Elvis to Engelbert What's-his-name. Not to mention every politician, casino owner, banker, and land developer in the state. And they all left a few pounds heavier and a few thousand lighter, if you know what I mean."

Meyer paused to rub his right earlobe between his thumb and index finger before saying, "And that's that. I invested a few shekels in downtown properties to keep my hand in the game, kibitzed around at golf, and took Ruthie to Israel more than once. All the while spending too much time at the goddamned doctor's. Basically, I was falling apart. Heart, kidneys, you name it. And one day I went to sleep and never woke up. At least," he paused, still rubbing his earlobe, "I think that's what happened. It's strange, the old days I remember clear as can be, but I couldn't tell you what I had for breakfast. If I ate breakfast, which I don't. But you get my drift."

I got it, all right. I'm certain my face dropped when I realized Meyer would be of no help solving the mystery of what befell him. Or why he'd come back. Or what any of this had to do with me. All I knew for sure was that he vanished one day without a trace. Theories sprouted like dandelions and were just as useful: everything from a long-delayed mob hit to a senile old man wandering off in the desert. Both involved abandoned mine shafts in one form or another, but that's where they parted ways. I was hoping Meyer himself would provide the answer, or at worst a clue, but it was not to be. At least not yet. Perhaps his more recent memories would return over time. But I couldn't just sit around and wait, no matter how much of a sloth I felt like. What I could do was put on my detective hat and pore over my transcript for something I might have missed. Because somewhere deep down, I knew Meyer held the key to everything.

As if I needed more motivation, Meyer sat back and said in an almost imperceptible voice, "I loved this place." Long pause as he studied the room, drinking in every last detail. "Still do."

CHAPTER 44

"How many dollars am I holding?" Boozer asked. For a moment, I could envision him as a little kid, a mischievous one at that. He held what looked to be five or six overlapping singles under my nose.

"I hate guessing games," I said, pushing his hand away. "And get that nasty money away from me. It's full of germs. Especially in this town. You have no idea where it's been."

"Oh, I have an idea," he said. "Come on, take a guess. Just this once." He looked like Oliver pleading for more. And, of course, I caved. "If I play along, will you go away?"

He made the sign of the cross. "Swear to God."

I did a quick silent count. "Six. Now leave."

"Ha! Gotcha. It's two." He opened his palm to show me the intricate folding pattern that made two dollars look like three times that amount.

Against my better judgment, I said, "And this is important why?"

Boozer beamed like the Luxor. "Thought you'd never ask. Because when I give money to a valet,

I want him to think I'm a stand-up guy. After he sticks the bills in his pocket, it mixes with his other money and he'll never figure it out. So I get all the good karma without having to pay for it."

"There's only one drawback," I said. "You don't own a car."

"It's good to be prepared. Same reason I'm learning the alphabet backwards. Want to hear?"

"No."

"It's in case I get pulled over for drunk driving. I can trick them into thinking I'm sober. I've also been practicing how to walk a straight line with my eyes closed."

"Wouldn't it be easier simply not to drink and drive?"

He lapsed into a brief silence before saying, "Never crossed my mind. You're a real downer, you know that?"

"I do my best. Now live up to your end of the bargain and scram."

"Scram? Seriously? Who talks like that?"

Before I could answer, Lucky, who'd been snoring softly under the table, emitted a low growl, leaped to his feet in one fluid motion, and was out the doggie door in three bounds, Boozer following close behind, moving surprisingly fast for a man his size, grabbing the baseball bat we kept by the front door, and yelling over his shoulder, "Stay put! This shit just got real!"

In the seconds that followed, everything happened at once: blood-curdling snarls, a high-pitched scream, a string of expletives, three short pop-pop-pops, the clang of our wrought-iron gate.

And then silence, in its own way even more ominous than what preceded it.

No longer able to ignore Boozer's admonition, I hoisted myself up, wobbled to the door, and stuck my head out into the crisp night air.

"Boozer! Lucky!" No sign. Venturing into the courtyard, I thought I heard Meyer's voice warn, Keep your eyes open. Go slow. As if I could move any other way. I nodded grimly, my senses on high alert. And beneath the surface, an aura of preternatural calm that surprised me most of all.

The scene lying before me could have been fashioned by a Hollywood set designer. A gas can and cloth leaning up against the house, the bloody remnants of a Nike sneaker, a stomach-churning jumble of hair and fur, a trail of red droplets leading out the now-open gate. And, as if pointing me in the right direction, a severed finger.

❧ CHAPTER 45 ❧

Boozer staggered back into the courtyard a few minutes later, soaked with sweat, hair plastered against his forehead in slimy black tendrils, and a high-pitched wheeze coming from his lungs every time he fought to catch his breath. Most troubling of all, a silver-dollar sized splotch of blood was spreading like a crimson oil slick just below his right collarbone. He leaned hard against a cinder-block pillar before sliding to a sitting position.

"My God, Boozer! Are you okay?"

"I think so, yeah. Let me just rest here for a minute."

A car whooshed by in front of the house, a reminder that, no matter how strange things got, life went on.

"What's with the blood?" I indicated a similar location on my own body in case he needed a clue.

Staring down in bewilderment at the red expanse now saturating the entire upper right quadrant of his formerly plain-white T, he pressed on the stain with the palm of his hand and flinched.

In a flat tone, Boozer said, “I hate to say it, but I think I’m shot.”

“What? Shot! Where’s my phone? Where is it, goddamn it? I’m calling nine-one-one.”

I turned toward the house to look for my cell when Boozer screeched, “Don’t!”

“What do you mean, don’t?”

“If you call Emergency, they’ll have a record of it and then we’ll need to tell Aaron and he’ll be really afraid for you and pissed off at me and he’ll make you sell the house and I know how much you love this place and …”

“What? You’re out of your mind! How pissed will Aaron be when he finds out I let his best friend and my roommate, who might’ve just saved our lives, bleed to death in the courtyard? You stay right there. An ambulance will be here soon.” I turned again to run into the house, but again he stopped me.

“Wait! Anna, please. Maybe this thing looks worse than it is. Maybe it’s just a flesh wound you can put a Band-Aid over. Please.”

I started to argue with him, but really, what could I say? If that’s what he wanted, who was I to go against his wishes? “Okay, let’s get you inside under the light and take a look. Can you stand?”

“Can I stand? Can I stand? Of course I can stand,” he said, pooh-poohing my concerns until he actually made an effort to accomplish the task. Fortunately, his aluminum bat (sporting, I noticed, a couple of new dings) lay within reach and he used it to boost himself into a locked and upright position.

Employing the bat as a cane and my shoulder for support, we lumbered to the nearest bathroom, the one just off the kitchen, with the clawfoot tub and purple floral velveteen wallpaper, lowering his mass onto the toilet while I ran to the master bath where I kept the first-aid kit.

After thoroughly scrubbing my hands and donning a pair of latex gloves, I said, "If this doesn't work, I'm depositing you at the nearest ER, no questions asked. Got it?"

"Sure. And thanks for checking it out. You know, my father had a string of doctor jokes. The funniest one had the punchline, 'When all else fails, examine the patient.'"

Just then, I emptied half a bottle of peroxide on the wound.

"Holy fucking shit! Why didn't you warn me?"

"Hey, I'm making this up as I go along. You're my first bullet wound." Daubing at the entry point with a clean towel, I was pleased to see a fragment of slug poking out from the ragged laceration.

"Looks like a twenty-two," I heard myself say. Or was it Meyer? "Shush! I'm trying to concentrate."

"I didn't say anything," Boozer said.

Ignoring him, I used an oversized tweezers to grasp the shard, pulling it out in one clean motion.

"Owww! Owww! Owww!"

"Got it," I said, proudly holding the spikey shrapnel up to the light with an unexpectedly steady hand. It looked like something that belonged on Dennis Rodman. I finished the patch job with a generous amount of antibiotic ointment, a large adhesive bandage, and half a roll of gauze. "Not bad, if I say so myself," I commented after peeling off the gloves and inspecting my handiwork. "You're lucky it was superficial. Looks like we've staunched the bleeding already. But we'd better keep an eye on it. If it gets infected, you'll need that trip to the hospital for sure." I stopped to think for a second. "We can tell them it was a fishing accident."

Boozer examined me with a suspicious eye. "Where'd you learn all that MASH shit?"

Honestly, I had no clue, but said, "I wrote an article a few years back. The info must have stayed with me. They say the subconscious never forgets anything. Maybe it's like the mom who gets a superhuman burst of strength, so she can lift a car off her children." Boozer seemed to buy it. I had to admit, this lying stuff was getting easier all the time.

When I finally allowed myself the luxury of sitting on the edge of the tub, exhaustion washed over me with tsunami force. "Man, I'm beat," I said.

"Tell me about it."

"Actually, you tell me about it. What the hell happened out there? And where's my dog, by the way?" I felt awful that I hadn't thought about Lucky until now. I guess the mind can only focus on one major crisis at a time.

"He's fine. At least I think so. That's some pooch you've got there. By the time I made it outside, he'd already gotten one asshole on the ground, clamping down on the guy's hand with those monster jaws, shaking him so hard I thought his arm might come off. You probably heard the screams. Meanwhile, the other dude, big ugly fuck, gets off three rounds before I could go all Louisville Slugger on his ass. One of the loads slams right into Lucky's head, point blank. And you know what happens?"

I shook my head, feeling dizzy.

Boozer continued, "Nothing. Absolutely nothing. The bullet literally bounces off his noggin. And into me, by the looks of it. Or at least a piece of it."

"No way!"

"Yes way. Meanwhile, these two douchebags take off on foot with Lucky hot on their heels, pissed off as hell, and me trailing badly behind. I see them jump into a black pickup halfway down the block and burn rubber, and Lucky's right on their asses. Might still be, for all I know."

"Well, I hope not," I said. Then I had a thought. "Hey, are you okay to drive?"

"I'm an excellent driver."

I shook my head. "I mean, are you up to it? Being shot and all."

"I don't see why not. I've driven more impaired than this."

"Good. Or not." I was never on solid ground talking to the big lug. "Could you go look for Lucky? Take some leftover turkey from the fridge. He loves turkey." I tossed him my car keys, which he caught, but groaned in pain.

"Damn!" he cried, rubbing his chest. "I'm gonna have to try to remember I've been shot."

I was worried I might've missed a fragment or two, or he had some internal damage.

"You're sure you're okay here alone?" he asked.

I suppose it should've occurred to me, but it hadn't. "No. I don't know. Maybe. You think they'll be back?"

"Probably not. I mean, they couldn't get away fast enough, right?"

I must have looked dubious or scared, because he was quick to add, "Anyways, I won't be gone long. I'm sure that mutt can smell meat a mile away. Right?"

I mustered a weak, "Right," then looked at my watch. "I figure we have about two hours to get this place cleaned up before Aaron gets home." Definitely not a job for an eight-month pregnant woman with an incompetent cervix, or even a fairly competent one. But what choice did I have? You do what needs to be done. And Boozer would be back soon to help. I hoped. "Either that," I continued, "or we've both got some 'splainin' to do."

"No doubt."

As he trundled off, I called out, "Hey, Boozer!"

He wheeled around in slow motion. "Yeah?"

"You did good tonight." Using bad grammar for effect.

The big man blew me a kiss. "That's how we does it."

CHAPTER 46

"Lucky!"
"Woof!"
"I love you, boy."
"Woof!"

CHAPTER 47

Aaron turned one of the dining room chairs around and saddled it like a horse. "We need to talk."

With a mixture of amusement and concern, I said, "Shouldn't that be my line?" A little test comment to gauge the gravity of the ensuing conversation.

"I'm serious," he confirmed with no suggestion of a smile. Uh-oh, I thought, and settled in for the long haul. Aaron continued, "I don't exactly know what's going on around here, but I can tell something's up. The new crease in Lucky's head, for example."

"I told you, he ran into the gate chasing one of the neighborhood cats. The big orange one."

Lucky raised his head with a whine, as if to say, "Who, me?"

Aaron was having none of it. "Well, I'm not so sure about that. I looked at it closely and there's some kind of burn mark where his fur used to be. The gate wouldn't do that. And I smelled gasoline fumes in the front yard when I came home last night. And just now I saw a couple of small dark-brown spots on the concrete. Meanwhile, Boozer's looking a little pale and playing even dumber than usual." He examined me with such intensity, I thought he could read not only my mind, but the baby's too. "Look, I'm worried about you, Anna. And I can't be of any help unless you tell me what's going on around here."

He leaned forward and stared directly into my eyes. After an uncomfortably long time that may have been 15 seconds, I buckled and spewed out the whole story from beginning to end, though I withheld the part about Meyer, of course. When I finished, the weight I'd been lugging around since last night floated away like so many helium balloons. And then, to my amazement, Aaron came to me and we hugged longer than we'd ever hugged. When we at last parted, he gently took my head in his hands and asked, "So what are we gonna do?" We. At that moment, the sweetest word I'd ever heard.

And then it all unraveled.

"How could you try to keep all this from me?" It was the first time Aaron had ever raised his voice to me. "The lives of my dog, my oldest friend, and my wife! Not to mention the baby. Our baby. All threatened! And I have to drag it out of you! Why?"

"Because we were afraid you'd want to sell the house!"

"And what person in his right mind wouldn't? Do you think I'd just shrug and go, oh well, if I came home and found the house burned to the ground and the three of you a pile of bones on the floor?"

"No! Of course not—"

"It almost happened once. I'm not gonna let it happen again."

"What do you mean?"

"I mean," he paused and glared at me, "I'm gonna sell this fucking house!"

I backed away like I'd just touched an electric fence, the anger rising up in volcanic proportions. But before I could explode, Aaron kept yelling.

"It's just a house! Chuck Caldwell's gone. And Ed Scott. Our only allies. Who knows what happened to them. These are bad people we're dealing with. Willing to do anything, by the looks of it. I'm done putting all our lives at risk. Including my boy's."

I drew a deep breath in an effort to fake my way through a rational reply.

"I can't believe what I'm hearing. These are bad people, you said so yourself. Bullies or worse. We can't just let them win. We brought this house back to life with our own hands. I love it here. I could see us staying forever, raising our family, growing old. I thought we were in this together. A team. I don't know about you, but I can't settle. I won't!" Me and not me at the same time. Feeling like a ventriloquist's dummy, powerless in every way.

"You can't believe what you're hearing? How do you think it sounds to me—that you're risking all of our lives! This isn't a game, Anna. It's not about winning and losing." He looked at me like he had no idea who I was. “You know, sometimes I think you love this house more than you love me.”

A woman can spend a fortune going for EKGs and stress tests and other heart exams. Or she can get in an argument like this with her significant other and feel her blood pressure set new altitude records. “You’re seriously going there? That’s so not fair. What I’m saying is we have to stand up for ourselves, draw a line in the sand. If we give up now, we’ll regret it, I know we will. You only get so many chances in life to do the right thing, find out what you’re made of.” Where had I heard that before? “This is our moment.”

“Are you nuts? What happened to the girl who burst into tears when a Dickweed told her no? When did she turn into Rambo?”

I just stood there, shaking in fury. One of us had crossed a line. Maybe both of us. And I wasn’t sure it could be uncrossed.

You know how quickly you can fall in love? That’s how fast you can fall out of it.

CHAPTER 48

Over the next two days, we passed in the hall a few times, but mainly stayed out of each other's way. Meyer's place was that big. You could play "Marco Polo" and never get a winner. My white-hot anger had settled into a seething burn, more appropriate for holding a forever grudge. Meanwhile, my brain kept skittering over contingency plans. Kick Aaron out? Run back to Michigan with my tail between my legs? Continue in this vein indefinitely?

On day three, as I sat at my desk researching cheap flights home, contemplating the prospect of the baby and me moving back into my old room forever, Aaron stepped in with a hangdog expression and his favorite acoustic guitar, the one that looked like Willie Nelson's face. Before I could protest, he began strumming a song in a sad minor key, accompanied by a voice at once sweet and sorrowful:

When you go away
You got nothin' to say
It's just another day.

Said I was your guy
Said you'd give it a try
Now it's a sad goodbye.

Come and take my hand
Before you head for the door
You want more, you want more.

Come and take my hand
Come and take my hand
You want more, you want more.

You look in my eyes
As the seconds tick by
Guess I had it all wrong
But why, oh why?

I remember the time
When you said you were mine
Was I really that blind?
That blind, that blind?

Come and take my hand ...

There was more, but that was the idea. Lyrics never have the same impact when you read them, without the music and the emotion. But he wrote it and sang it for me and that was what counted. I could tell he meant every word. Nobody had ever done that before. I could get used to being his muse.

When he finished, he stood there like a lost little boy, his eyes glistening, imploring me to give him one more chance. I'm sure my eyes matched his in the moisture department.

"You're right," he half-whispered. "We're in this together."

You know how quickly you can fall out of love? That's how fast you can fall back in.

CHAPTER 49

Meyer said, "I think I remember something about the house. Something important."

He'd appeared at our kitchen table not long after Aaron left for work, wearing the kind of tan corduroy blazer with elbow patches favored by old college professors and a red-checkered driving cap I might have seen in one of his press photos. I put down my spoon and looked up from my bowl of Cheerios, my pulse quickening. "Really?"

"Yes. I'm recalling a safe. I can't put my finger on it, but I have a feeling it has something you need."

Despite all our renovations, I'd never run across anything as big as a safe and thought Meyer might be might be thinking of another house in another time. Still, I pushed my chair away from the table, stood up, and followed him into the master bedroom, Lucky bringing up the rear. Sliding the door open to our big walk-in closet, I flicked on the light and headed right to where Meyer was pointing, all the way to the back next to the laundry hamper.

"Nothing here."

"Try lifting up that patch of carpet in the corner."

I did as directed and was astounded to find the black metal face of an ancient safe sunk flush into the cement floor. It displayed stencil-style lettering spelling out Diebold Safe & Lock Co., Canton, O, along with a combination dial and, incongruously, the painted image of an idyllic winter scene. It looked cold and impenetrable.

I glanced at Meyer, who looked quite proud of himself. "I knew it!" he said, doing a ghostly version of a fist pump.

I couldn't help getting caught up in his exuberance. "That's awesome, Meyer. What's the combo?"

He thought for a moment, looked up at the ceiling, tugged on his right ear, but none of his old magic could conjure up the numbers. "Damn it," was all he kept repeating, his shoulders slumped in defeat.

"No big deal. I'll just call a locksmith."

The only one I knew was Hometown Lock and Key, the hillbilly-looking serviceman who had responded to the officer's request at Mr. Caldwell's. I looked up the number and called, expecting to leave a message in the hope he could squeeze us in later in the week. Much to my surprise, he answered on the first ring.

"Hometown Lock."

I stammered, "Uh, I just found a safe in my floor, in the closet actually, and it's important I see what's inside, but we're new here and I don't know the combo, long story, and I know it's late but ..."

"So it's a mystery."

"I guess you could say that."

"I love a good mystery. One of the reasons I got into this line of work in the first place. Gimme your address and I'll be right over."

I felt like I just found a twenty in the laundry.

Less than a half-hour later, the locksmith, Kenny by the name embroidered on his blue work shirt, shuffled up the walkway toting the same beat-up rusted green toolbox I'd seen previously. After brief re-introductions, in which I reminded him we'd sort of met before and I assured him Lucky wouldn't rip his lungs out, Meyer and I ushered him to the rear of the closet.

"Let me ask you something," Kenny said. "Do you want to use the safe again? If so, I can listen through a stethoscope while I manipulate the dial. Real old-school stuff I don't get to do that often. But it'll probably take a good hour or so. If not, I can drill this baby open in no time, but it'll leave a mess and the safe won't work properly without being repaired. But I won't ruin it, either, which would be a shame, because this one's a beauty." He stepped back and looked me straight in the eyes. "Your call."

"Let's go with the drill," I said, and saw Meyer nod in agreement.

True to his word, Kenny drilled a small hole in the safe, inserting a thin probe that he wiggled around for a few minutes before opening the door effortlessly. Meyer and I leaned forward in anticipation, staring into the bowels of the safe, which appeared ... empty. To make sure, Kenny pointed a strong flashlight beam into the void, revealing a thin layer of dust, some dead bugs (how they got in there, I'll never know), and a yellowed piece of notebook paper folded into a tight square.

"Sorry to disappoint you," Kenny said. "This happens more than you'd think. I still need to charge you the standard rate."

"No problem," I said, writing him a check, thanking him, and seeing him off, disappointed in yet another dead end.

When I got back to the bedroom, Meyer was as corporeal as I'd ever seen him. "That's it!" he cried. I'd never heard him so excited. Before I lost my nerve, I reached in to retrieve the paper, unfolding it as quickly as I dared without accidentally tearing the aged document to ribbons.

The paper contained a faded and nearly indecipherable hand-drawn pencil sketch of what could only be some sort of schematic, with wires and numbers and letters leading in and out of four rectangular objects of various sizes. I couldn't begin to envision what it represented or why it mattered, but I had a strong feeling that Meyer would explain. I made a conscious attempt to remain calm as I contemplated the crude diagram that held, perhaps, the key to everything.

Over my shoulder, Meyer examined the drawing a long time with something approaching reverence, finally breaking the silence. "I always wondered where that went. You have no idea how many times I turned this place upside down looking for it."

"What is it?"

"Directions for hooking up my hi-fi. Now I can listen to my Dave Brubeck LPs."

I had no idea what hi-fi was. Or who Dave Brubeck was, for that matter. All I knew for sure was that the little piece of paper was of no help whatsoever. Still, Meyer was happy. And that counted for something, I guess.

As for me, I had some homework to do.

CHAPTER 50

I went to bed discouraged, no closer to understanding what was going on than the day Meyer and I crossed paths for the first time. Fortunately, exhaustion won out and I quickly fell into a bottomless sleep, never completing a single toss or turn. Hours later, with Aaron still at work but well before dawn, I awoke to see the old ghost standing at the foot of the bed, looking almost like a real man, not a specter at all. Staring at me in wide-eyed wonder, he said in a surprisingly strong voice, "I remember everything."

Finally.

O

I called Pykowski first thing in the morning, although I had to go through eight layers of flunkies to get to him. Each time, I said some variation of, "This is Anna Eisenberg calling for Mr. Pykowski. No, I won't leave a message. He'll want to talk to me, I guarantee it. Just tell him it's me, before he hears that you wouldn't put me through to him and he fires you. Yes, I'll hold."

Each time the automated system subjected me to ads for the Mile High Buffet ("… 99 hot and cold items for $9.99"), the Moist Lounge ("… featuring the swingin' sounds of Funk Box with a two-drink minimum") and Climax! ("… the screaming bungee plunge from our 1,100-foot platform"), interspersed with electronica music that was current when I was in junior high.

Finally, after yet another "Please hold," a chilling male voice came on the line. "Anna. So good to hear from you. I'd almost given up hope."

I prayed he didn't notice the involuntary gulp that sounded to my own ears like something from a Saturday-morning cartoon. It took me a few seconds to collect myself.

"Mr. Pykowski," I said in what I hoped was a flat unemotional tone. "I'm ready to settle up."

CHAPTER 51

"Behold the French fry, nature's most perfect food," Bob Pykowski said to me as I entered his office through heavy double doors. Of all the opening lines I could have expected, this didn't make my top million. He snagged a fry from the mound in front of him, held it up triumphantly, and fixed it with a lover's gaze. "Crisp on the outside, tender on the inside, with a satisfying saltiness that just begs for another. And another. I could live on these babies."

And die on them, I thought. The sooner the better.

I gave his office the once-over. Everything about it screamed egomaniac, from the too-plush gold carpeting and the meticulously arranged football, basketball, and golf trophies to the eight-by-ten framed photos of Pykowski himself towering over the last three Nevada governors. Not to mention the centerpiece, an enormous floor-to-ceiling tank stocked with colorful tropical fish and anchored by what looked like a small shark circling frenetically, the vestige of a striped tail dangling from its mouth.

Pykowski polished off the tater and licked his lips. "No ketchup," he said, as if I cared. "I'm a purist." Pushing the oversized plate in my direction, he added, "Care to join me?"

I waved him off. The thought of sharing anything with him made me sick, and the idea of food, let alone greasy fast-food French fries, turned my stomach inside out. As did the sour odor permeating the room, perhaps an extension of whatever was going on in Pykowski's head.

He writhed up from behind his massive desk and extended a fleshy paw, which is when I noticed he wore nothing but a ratty faded blue terrycloth robe with more holes than fabric, two white hairless legs sticking out from the bottom like pipe cleaners. I found myself praying his minimalist ensemble included underwear.

"So you're Anna Eisenberg," he said, looking me up and down appraisingly. The fine hair on my arms stood on end and I shuddered despite myself. "I feel as if I know you."

Ignoring the hand, I said, "And I you." He stood there for an awkward moment before settling back into an executive chair that could have been purchased at the Sultan of Brunei's garage sale. Up close and personal, Pykowski didn't seem nearly as intimidating as I had imagined—just another ex-jock gone to fat, probably from too much booze (and French fries), if the well-stocked bar and spider veins on his nose were any indication.

"Please sit," he said. "A woman in your condition ..."

"Shouldn't be here at all," I said, thankful the doctor's protocol had kept my contractions at bay. "I'll stand, thank you." And just like that, the butterflies in my stomach flew off to bother someone else. Maybe Pykowski could sense the shift as he ran a hand through his head of pinkish orange hair, the residue of a dye job gone horribly wrong.

"When are you due?" he asked. You had to hand it to the guy; he was nothing if not persistent.

"Any minute now, which is why I need to speak my piece and get out of here."

Pykowski didn't say another word. Instead, he slid open the top drawer of his desk and extracted a checkbook bound in the hide of an animal possibly on the verge of extinction. Opening it with a flourish, he extracted a gold fountain pen from his pocket and held it over the page. "I'm prepared to write you a check in the amount of, shall we say, seven hundred thousand dollars."

I shook my head. "The house isn't for sale."

The blood drained from his face. "Huh? I thought we were settling up."

"We are."

I stood my ground, focusing on the twitch in his left eye, a surefire tell in this game of high-stakes poker.

"Eight hundred thousand," he said.

"No."

"I don't know what kind of bait and switch you're pulling here, missy." A real edge to his voice now. "Everything's for sale. A million dollars. My final offer. That's more than someone like you and that husband of yours could possibly hope to make in a lifetime."

My face went white hot. "Maybe you should listen when someone talks to you," I said softly, determined to keep my composure. I knew that the first one who snapped would be the loser.

The color of his face matched my own and little beads of sweat popped out on his forehead, just as the air conditioner cycled on with a low thrum. "Now you listen to me," he said, the salesman's velvet tones replaced by a menacing hiss. "We can do this the easy way or we can do it the hard way."

"Is that how you did it with Mr. Caldwell?" Although I hadn't seen the body personally, an image of my neighbor's lifeless form surged into view.

"Lucky break. For me," he said with a chuckle. Short pause, then, "You have no idea who you're dealing with."

"Oh, I have an idea all right. Ever since your goons tried to burn down my house."

Pykowski harrumphed. "Oh, please. I just meant to scare you. If I wanted you dead, you'd be dead."

"Like Ed Scott?"

"Scott drowned. Don't you read the paper?"

In that instant, I felt a seismic shift as my consciousness stepped aside, replaced by that of a diminutive Jewish racketeer now solely in the driver's seat. Leaning over the desk, I/he said, "I've had enough of you, you spineless little putz," in a voice peppered with Meyer's trademark inflections. "You're not the man your father was, not by a long shot. Want to know the truth? He was always disappointed in you. He'd say to me, 'The kid's soft. Takes after his mother. He'll never amount to anything.' And he was right."

Confusion settled around Pykowski's face and he stopped chewing mid-fry. "Now where in the world did you read that?"

Meyer stormed ahead. "I was there, remember?"

"Where? What?"

"Just you. Your father. And me. In the basement of the Lewis & Clark, right under my casino. Your old man was a heartless bastard, but at least he was someone I could respect. Self-made, pulled himself up by the bootstraps like we all did in those days. And there he is, angling for controlling interest in the joint, because he thinks I'm too old, I've lost my touch. And I won't budge an inch, despite all the threats. Because I've lived my life, you know? And he says I'd better play ball or I could experience, how did he put it? 'Sudden death.' I start to laugh, really hard, tears running down my cheeks. He stares at me like I've lost my mind and I say, 'At my age, it's not so sudden.' And he laughs, too. Right before he backhands me across the mouth. And I taste blood, not for the first time, I can tell you that. And I say, 'There's nothing you can do to me that someone hasn't already done worse. Like the doctor who did my last prostate exam."

While Meyer stopped to collect his thoughts,

I noticed Pykowski sitting there with his mouth agape, staring straight ahead at a scene taking place in a different room thirty years distant.

Clearing his throat, Meyer picked up the narrative. "And you, you're standing back of your old man like you always did, playing pocket pool and looking like you're gonna piss your pants. You couldn't have been more than what, sixteen, seventeen, tops? And he looks at you and says, 'Bobby, I'm going to make a man out of you if it kills me.' And he reaches into his waist band and tries to hand you a twenty-two, the Smith and Wesson with the wood grip. But you want no part of it, like it's a hot coal or something, and you start to back away. That's when your father says, 'Take it or so help me I will knock your fuckin' teeth out.' And all the color drains from your face and you finally reach for it and your hand closes around the gun and I can see a little tear trickle down your cheek. Your father sees it too and yells, 'Don't you cry, you little shit, or I'll give you something to really cry about!' Spit flying everywhere, his eyes black and dead, and he starts barking out instructions.

"'Point it at his face. Do it!' And you do as you're told, you raise the gun, but your hand is quaking like you've got some kind of palsy, and your father turns to me and says, 'I'm going to count to ten and if you don't sign the papers, Bobby Junior here is going to make me very proud. Aren't you, boy?'

"And you manage to squeal out a little 'Yes sir,' but I can tell you don't mean it, you can't do it. And I say to your old man, 'I didn't know you could count that high.' I'm not afraid. I've got emphysema and heart trouble, I'm seventy-nine, for Chrissake, almost eighty. Which is long enough. And my Ruthie is halfway to senility anyway and barely knows me; she's in the nursing home I built with my own two hands. And I look right at you and say, 'Go ahead, Bobby. You'll be doing me a favor.' And your father is already at five, six, seven, and you look like you're about to throw up, eight, nine ... And I'm ready, but then, looking at you, through you, right into your God-forsaken soul, I'm thinking maybe I'll catch a break and see my Ruthie again. And your father screams, 'Ten! Shoot him! Shoot him! Shoot the old son-of-a-bitch!'"

Meyer paused. This was using up the last bit of ghost energy that remained to him, though he also seemed to be relishing the retelling as he picked up the thread.

"But you just stand there, frozen, sobbing like a baby, a yellow puddle pooling around your feet, and your father finally grabs your hand, just seizes it, wraps his own hand around it, and together you're aiming the gun at me and he says, 'Last chance,' to which I say, 'Fuck you.' I don't even flinch. And those are my final words in this world, because the next thing I know, I'm waking up in this young lady's house, my house, and if you really want the house, this time you're going to have to kill me yourself."

He stopped again, catching his breath, then said, "I'm betting you won't, because you still haven't got the *beystim*, the balls."

The part of me that wasn't Meyer, that was still me, understood he was gambling with my very existence and I should have been scared to death, not to mention royally pissed. What right did he have to do that? But I also knew, deep down, that Meyer wasn't gambling at all. It wasn't his nature. The house never gambles; it just grinds. Owning a casino is the closest you can get to a sure thing. And so was this. I gazed deep into Pykowski's vacant eyes and all traces of doubt disappeared.

Reaching across his desk, I grabbed a cold fry and jammed it in my mouth, establishing my territory, saying in my own voice, "I'm leaving now. If you want to shoot me, you'll have to do it yourself. In the back. Because Daddy's not here to bail you out anymore."

Turning on my heels, I headed for the door, but not before an improvised moment of brilliance prompted me to pluck a golf club (a wood?) out of his bag and slam it with all my pent-up rage into the side of the fish tank. For a micro-second nothing happened, except for the stabbing pain radiating up to my elbows and bringing water to my eyes. And then a tiny crack appeared in the glass, followed by another and another, spreading like a virus, and then a different kind of crack, a thunderous boom that made the shark stop circling and stare at me like it knew what was about to happen, just before the mini-tidal wave swept him and the rest of the tank's contents all over the too-plush carpeting. The gasping flopping creatures triggered a twinge of regret, but they were Pykowski's problem now; with any luck, the shark would latch onto him with those razor teeth and do serious damage to something important.

Facing Pykowski one final time, I couldn't resist a parting shot. "You, of all people, should know. The house always wins."

Every molecule in me wanted to run. Instead, I forced myself to saunter out those big double doors, savoring the man's last moments of feigned bravado as he screamed, "Don't you walk out on me! Nobody walks out on Bob Pykowski! We're not through until I say we're through!" Trying to salvage some shred of self-respect. But I could tell his heart wasn't in it.

And I knew he would never bother us again.

Then I was halfway down the hall, closing in on the elevator as three of Pykowski's security detail, one with a huge bandage encasing his hand, charged past me, so close I could feel the draft, Pykowski's tortured howl trailing off in the distance.

As the elevator doors closed around me, wrapping me in their protective cocoon, I felt my shoulders unclench and finally allowed myself a tight humorless smile. Too much had happened for much more; maybe I'd celebrate in a day or a week or a month. For now, all I could do was emit a soft, "Thank you, Meyer," in a rasp that didn't sound like me at all.

And that was when my water broke.

EPILOGUE

Neither Aaron nor I being synagogue-goers, we found our *mohel* on Yelp. (Insert joke here.) I'd gone from never even hearing the word *bris* to participating in one in record time, after, of course, going through the Wikipedia crash course.

A *bris*, or technically *bris milah*, is the covenant of circumcision, a physical symbol of the relationship between God and the Jewish people dating back 4,000 years. According to the Old Testament, God commanded the patriarch Abraham to circumcise himself, his 13-year-old son Isaac, and his other male followers as a sign of their special pact. You'd think that Abraham, a spry 99 at the time, would have met his share of resistance, but apparently his pals were a trusting bunch and the idea somehow caught on. Today, a circumcised penis is what all the best-coiffed Jews are wearing and in my limited experience, most of the *goyishe* men too. Of course, today the ceremony is followed by a nice party, which gives family and friends, especially the males in attendance, a chance to untighten their sphincter muscles and relax with a glass of wine. Or three.

For some unknown reason, the Torah mandates that the whole megillah take place on the eighth day after birth. And whereas the father performed it back in the day, now it's done by a circumcision specialist called a *mohel*, much to Aaron's relief. Enter Yelp.

We naturally picked the guy with the most stars who also doubled as an MD with more than 2,000 circumcisions under his belt (so to speak). Why take any chances, right? We especially liked the review that said, "Our son has had absolutely no complications and our pediatrician said everything looks 'perfect.'" Sounded like $500 well-spent.

I don't know what I was expecting when Barry Kaplan came to the door for our briefing (and, in Aaron's words, the "ritualistic handing over of the check"), but he looked nothing like the guy from *Fiddler on the Roof*. Tall, athletic, youngish, with curly black hair and a kind face, he answered all our questions and allayed our fears, providing a step-by-step game plan of what to expect, which included, toward the end, giving our baby his Hebrew name.

"What have you decided? In English?" he asked me.

"Michael Joshua. Michael, because we like how it sounds. And Joshua after my husband's best friend, who, it just so happens, saved my life. Long story."

Kaplan smiled and said, "I'd enjoy hearing it

someday. So Michael Joshua it is." He wrote it down in his appointment book and paused to sip his coffee. "Any thoughts on what to name him in Hebrew? Trust me, you'll only call him that as a bar mitzvah. And when he's in trouble."

Aaron and I exchanged a look. "We're kind of out of our league here," he said.

"Well, we could have a long drawn-out discussion," Kaplan said. "Or I could surprise you."

❧O☙

Aaron's circumcision fears didn't stay allayed for long. "Are you awake?" he asked me the morning of the ceremony.

Shaking the cobwebs from my brain, I muttered, "I am now."

"I was thinking."

"Uh-oh."

"No, seriously." He rolled over to face me, delivering a blast of morning breath. "I've been doing some research. Many people, even Jews, are getting away from the whole circumcision thing. They say it's a barbaric custom, completely unnecessary. Some cultures even see it as a sign of mutilation. I mean, if God's so perfect, why would he create something that needs to be cut off?"

"No idea. I'm new to this party, remember?"

"So you're okay if we cancel?"

I stuck out my hand traffic cop-style, briefly admiring the custom gold wedding band that looked an awful lot like a plastic straw, and said, "Cool your jets, Turbo. I didn't say that. Listen, I know it's tough for you men, walking around with that thing between your legs calling all the shots. But we can't have little Michael looking like an outcast in the school locker room, lumped in with all the German exchange students."

"They don't make kids take showers anymore."

"Don't interrupt, I'm riffing here. Or worse yet, getting some kind of infection. Know what your problem is? Too much empathy. I get it. But this looks like cold feet, plain and simple."

"Cold something," Aaron agreed.

I took his hand in mine and looked him square in the eye. "Honey, we're Jewish. Can't we just act like it?"

~O~

My mother, granted the honor of carrying Michael from the bedroom to the living room on an oversized satin blue-and-white *bris* pillow, laid him gently in the lap of my father, who had been granted the even greater (albeit dubious) honor of holding our little fella during the actual procedure. I had to admit, my father looked just this side of scared, something I'd never seen from him before; perhaps this whole empathy thing was more pervasive than I initially thought. If I could read his mind, which I sort of could, he was surely thinking, I traveled 2,000 miles across the country for this?

Having delivered the goods, my mother smoothed her dress and took her place on a folding chair alongside the rest of our small circle of friends and well-wishers: Boozer; Rob Lazarus, the other ex-bandmates, and their significant others; the attorney Marty Rosen; Libby Silver, our Realtor; and the lead singer from Meltdown. Lucky, although a full-fledged member of the family, was relegated to watching from the back yard through the sliding glass door, for fear he might contaminate the proceedings or decide to nosh on a rare treat. Yes, dogs, even heroic ones, can be disgusting.

Missing, more or less, was Auntie, who had hurt her back shoveling snow, but was joining us via Skype. And, sadly, Mr. Caldwell and Ed Scott, who I would always believe paid the ultimate price for their involvement and whose absence cast a pall over my own personal festivities. Had it been worth it? That was a conversation with myself for another day. For now, as I looked at the faces of my newborn son, his father (rocking his newly minted music-producer's haircut), and our loved ones in this special gathering place, the joy washing over me obliterated all doubts.

And then there was Meyer, who had never returned to the house after our confrontation with Pykowski. Although I missed his oddly comforting presence, I had a feeling he had completed his journey and was free to move on. (Or maybe I had simply regained my sanity.) Wherever he was now, I hoped he found peace. Maybe even happiness. And Ruthie.

The day's business brought my mind back into focus. "We're ready to begin the ceremony," Dr. Kaplan announced cheerfully, lighting two candles on either side. "We kindle the light to honor new life in the presence of God." Playing softly in the background, Dave Brubeck's "Time Out" provided the soundtrack for our occasion.

I saw my father dip a gauze into a chalice of Manischewitz wine, the sickeningly sweet Concord grape potion Jews save for special occasions like this, and give it to little Michael to suck on. Although our *mohel* had recommended only a drop or two, I could see the look of relief on Aaron's and my father's faces when it appeared to put our son under as fast as any operating-room anesthetic. My father followed it by downing a big purple chaser himself, eliciting an immediate wince and, in all probability, a headache for later, before passing the goblet to Aaron to do the same. All wholly inappropriate, to be sure, although Dr. Kaplan, to his credit, pretended not to notice.

"*Baruch ha-ba,*" said Dr. Kaplan. "Blessed is the one who has arrived." He then recited a Hebrew blessing with a lot of guttural Klingon sounds before turning to Aaron, who stood next to him, playing the part of scrub nurse and looking like he'd rather be cleaning a septic tank. With a shaky hand, Aaron picked up a clamp specifically designed to perform the deed with a minimum of pain and bleeding and offered it to the good doctor. Before diving right in, Dr. Kaplan talked a bit about the origins of the ceremony and the importance of raising Michael Joshua in a Jewish home.

Upon mention of this, I tried to catch Aaron's eye, but he was too far gone. Ascertaining that there were no questions, the doc suggested we close our eyes and pray for the well-being of the child. Of course, my pesky reporter's curiosity got the better of me and I peeked as he deftly performed the procedure that, surprisingly, took less than a minute and, not surprisingly, ended with the loudest shray I'd ever heard from a human being, let alone a newborn. At that moment, I might as well have had a penis of my own, the empathy flowing like wine and making me want to swoop in and spirit my baby away to another dimension. Before I could muster the nerve, the screaming stopped as quickly as it had begun, just as our mohel had predicted.

Swaddling him loosely in a diaper and asking us to pray for a speedy recovery, he handed Michael to me to take his rightful place in my arms. And all was right with the world.

"*L'chaim*!" Dr. Kaplan shouted. "To life!"

"Let's eat!" Boozer replied.

Our *mohel* laughed. "Not just yet. There's still the matter of Michael Joshua's Hebrew name to consider. Conferring this name is one of the most meaningful portions of the *bris milah* ceremony, because it will serve as the foundation of Michael's Jewish identity. Our most fervent hope is that this baby will grow to live a life of Torah, devoted relationships, and *tikkun olam*, literally 'repairing the world,' which is the obligation of every Jew. After all, part of living in this world is giving back to the world. Having been given the privilege of helping set this beautiful soul on his spiritual path, it is clear to me that he possesses unique gifts that could only come from our Creator. And so, I bestow upon him the name of Meir Yeshua. Meir for 'One Who Gives Light.' And Yeshua for 'Deliverer.'"

He gave Michael a few more drops of wine and said another prayer, but my brain was already reeling. It was as if I'd been permitted a glimpse behind a mysterious curtain into life's inner workings. The goose bumps were all the proof I needed. Meyer? Really? What were the odds of that?

~O~

Later, after our guests retired to their respective homes and rooms, and with Aaron sacked out on the sofa, it was just the baby and I in a rocking chair my father had crafted by hand (in record time) as a surprise gift.

As we moved back and forth to the ticking of the clock, I couldn't take my eyes off Michael's sweet little face, so perfect and innocent it made my soul ache. "Well, baby boy," I said through the lump in my throat, "it's been quite a week. What do you think of your new digs?"

By way of reply, he fixed his gaze on mine, following it with the cutest little cooing sound. And reached up to rub his right ear.

About the Author

Brian Rouff was born in Detroit, raised in Southern California, and has lived in Las Vegas since 1981, which makes him a long-timer by local standards. When he's not writing articles, screenplays, and Las Vegas-based novels such as *Dice Angel* and *Money Shot*, he runs Imagine Communications, a marketing and public relations firm in Henderson. Brian is married with two daughters and five grandchildren.

Brian can be reached at brouff@weareimagine.com.

❧ Author's Note ❧

The house depicted in this novel is based on an actual home my family and I lived in and remodeled from 2003 to 2005.

Sadly, it burned to the ground in 2014, long after we sold it and moved away. Today, it exists only in a handful of photographs.

And now in this book.